STRIPPING

and other stories

pagan kennedy

STRIPPING

and other stories

SERPENT'S TAIL

HIGH RISK

BOOKS

NEW YORK / LONDON

"Elvis's Bathroom" has appeared in the *Village Voice* and *Disorderly Conduct* (Serpent's Tail, 1991); "The Dead Rabbit Pocket" has appeared in *The Quarterly*; "Stripping," "Shrinks," and "Camp" have appeared in the *Village Voice*; "UFOs" has appeared in *The Quarterly* and *Story Quarterly*; "The Monument" has appeared in *Prairie Schooner*.

This collection first published 1994 by
High Risk Books/Serpent's Tail
4 Blackstock Mews, London, England N4 2BT
and 401 West Broadway, New York, NY 10012

Library of Congress Cataloging-in-Publication Data:
Kennedy, Pagan, 1962–
      Stripping, and other stories / Pagan Kennedy
                 p.   cm.
      ISBN 1-85242-322-6
      1. Young women—United States—Fiction. I. Title.
      PS3561.E4269s77   1994
      813'.54—dc20   93-35690
                                       CIP

British Library Cataloguing-in-Publication Data:
      Kennedy, Pagan
      Stripping, and other stories.—(High Risk)
      I. Title II. Series

Cover and book design by Rex Ray
Printed in Hong Kong by Colorcraft, Ltd.
        10 9 8 7 6 5 4 3 2

Thanks to the members of my writers' group for editing my manuscripts, hot gossip, lending me lots of laundry soap and generally watching out for me.

Contents

Elvis's Bathroom

ON ELVIS TV specials they tell you he "passed away," makes it sound like he died in bed. Truth is, Elvis died on the can, then he fell on the floor and curled up like a bug. Great, huh? The king of rock and roll dead on the floor with his pants around his ankles.

I never would've found out about that, or any of the cool stuff I found out about, if I hadn't got my tattoo. We'd just hitched to New York, my bullet-headed boyfriend and me, out two days of high school to see a band play. Before the concert we were hanging out in the park and I fell asleep—must've been the shit pot we'd bought. I had this dream about an upside-down Jesus hanging on an upside-down cross. Jesus's lips were all covered with spit and blood and I thought he was saying, "You got to stop ignoring me, Spike."

After the concert, me and my boyfriend went down by the docks—where the slaughterhouses are and it smells like fish—and into one of those all-night tattoo places. Underneath the eagles and naked ladies and anchors hung up over the counter is this tall guy with his eyebrows grown together.

I said I wanted that one on the wall, the cross, only upside-down and with no Jesus on it.

He goes, "Look, kid, I only do what you see up there. I ain't no artist." Then he started telling me what a bitch a tattoo is to get off—but actually that's why I wanted one. When I had the dream, I knew this upside-down Jesus was my Jesus, and he wanted me to do the coolest stuff, like stay in New York and be in a band instead of hitching back to New Hampshire the next day.

But I couldn't figure out how to stay in New York, cause I didn't know anyone. So getting the tattoo was like a pact with the upside-down Jesus.

The guy's hand was on the counter, and I put my hand on his and went, "Aw, mister, aw, pretty please?"

So he finally said okay, and let me up on the chair, which looked like a dentist's chair, except that it was all stained with dark brown spots, maybe dried blood. The guy worked slow, one dot at a time and each one felt like a tiny cigarette burn on my arm. The tattoo didn't look like anything at first, but when it was finished it was just like I wanted. And I was thinking that's how my life would be if I followed the upside-down Jesus—one cool thing after the other, and later I'd see how all along it'd fit together.

A YEAR LATER, when I'd just gotten out of high school, I was thinking I'd try to move to New York. Then this friend of mine who went to my school in New Hampshire, but a year ahead of me—Oona— called. She was living in the seedy part of Boston, where the hard-core and garage scene was. She said they needed someone in her house.

I went down for a day to look and the place was just my style: graffiti with the names of bands like UFO Baby and Reptile Head (Oona said they used to practice in the basement), stolen gravestone leaning against the banister on the staircase, big plastic Santa with a gas mask out on the porch, and in the kitchen, a bunch of chairs they obviously got off the sidewalk on trash day.

When Oona and me got to the bathroom, I saw this upside-down crucifix hanging from the chain you pull to make the toilet flush. Seeing that made me realize I wasn't supposed to go to New York at all.

I want, "Oona, check it out—just like on my arm," and I showed her my tattoo. I wanted her to see this was something amazing, cause for me it was a sign that I should live in this house.

She went, "That's all over the place in this neighborhood. It's a witchcraft thing." Oona's never freaked out by anything. She's great—a real curvy girl with long black hair, wears old lace dresses, smells sweet as a graveyard.

She started telling me about the house. What really freaked me out was that Juan Hombre, who used to be

3

with the Benign Tumors, still lived in the living room. They didn't make him pay rent cause he was a celebrity. Even living up in New Hampshire, I'd heard of the Tumors. They'd do covers of songs like "Going to the Chapel," first straight, like they were a '50s lounge band, and then they'd let loose on their own version and everyone watching would tear each other apart. Just when they were starting to get airplay, they broke up.

They put out one record, which I had. I couldn't even believe I owned it, it was so cool. On the back of the jacket was a picture of each Tumor. In Juan Hombre's he was jumping off the stage, twisted up in the air like a wrung-out rag—a skinny guy with heavy cheekbones, dark skin and wild black hair. He was the coolest-looking one of all of them. And when I thought of that picture again, I realized he looked like the upside-down Jesus in my dream.

I met him the day I moved in; there he was, sitting at the kitchen table, eating bread and reading the *New York Post*. He looked like a vampire, skinny as hell with dark circles under his eyes.

I told him I was the new girl moving in and sat down. I go, "I loved that record you guys put out."

"Thanks," he said, but he seemed embarrassed. I go, "So, is your name really Juan Hombre?"

He said, making fun of himself, "No that's my stage name. My real name's Mark Martinez, and I'm not even Spanish, just a Portugee boy."

I go, "What?"

"Portuguese—you know, sausages, sweet bread, cork farmers."

I WAS SPENDING a lot of time in the kitchen, wailing away on this African drum I had.

Juan would come in there a lot to get things—a beer or something—but then he'd sit down at the table and we'd start talking. Mostly we talked about Elvis. Me and Juan didn't give a shit about the early Elvis; we were into the late Elvis, like what he ate—fried peanut butter, bacon and banana sandwiches—and all the pills he took.

Before I met Juan, I didn't even know anything about Elvis. I thought he was supposed to be like Pat Boone. But we'd sit there at the kitchen table, and Juan would tell me Elvis stories. When Elvis didn't like a TV show, he'd take his cool-looking gun out of his belt and shoot out the TV; he stayed in his hotel room in Vegas where they brought him new TVs all the time. He could swallow sixteen pills at once. He'd get all these girls to strip down to their underwear and wrestle on top of the bed, and he'd sit on the floor watching. He called his dick "Little Elvis."

The weirdest shit was about how Elvis died: like, when they did the autopsy on him, they practically found a drugstore in his stomach, but the thing is, though, creepy thing is, none of the pills were digested. What I'm saying is, Elvis didn't die from pills like everyone thinks; he died from something else.

Before the end, he did a lot of reading—right there on the can. He got real religious, but in an Elvis way, reading stuff about UFO cults, Voodoo, Atlantis, raising people from the dead, same time as he was reading the Bible and considering himself some kind of big Christian.

Anyways, just after Juan told me about how Elvis died, I had this dream about him sitting in the bathroom reading—this book just like the Bible only it's the other Bible and it tells about Elvis's own Jesus. Elvis says some words out loud from the book and this other Jesus comes in through the door. He's a skeleton, with flames all around his bones and skull. The skeleton-Jesus touches Elvis on the forehead with one flaming finger, and that's when Elvis dies.

I said to Juan, "I want to go to Graceland. I feel like if I could just see his bathroom, I'd have a revelation or something." I was afraid to ask him to come, but then he said, "Yeah, let's do it. When do you want to go?" Our trip to Graceland—we talked about it a lot, but I think it was really just a way of saying we wanted to sleep together.

A COUPLE DAYS later, Juan asked me out on a "Date with Hombre," as he called it. We went to Deli-King—the diner where all the punks and street people hang out—and it was amazing being in there with him. We could barely get to a table, what with at least six people going, "Hey, Juan, where been? We missed you, man," and they all want to talk to him. The only ones who didn't recognize him were the real hard-core street people—only thing they talk to is their coffee.

Meat Hook, crazy fucker and former star of UFO Baby, stood up and clapped Juan on the back. He was tall and skinny with his hair in a greasy ponytail and a skull tattooed on his forehead. "Juan," he said, "we got a room open in our house. You want to live on Ashford?"

"Right now I'm okay," Juan said as we sat down. Juan was so cool I could practically see an aura around him; I couldn't believe it was me there in the booth with him. He was wearing a leather jacket someone had given him, just like that, cause they liked the Tumors. His hands stuck out of the sleeves, brown and bony with scars all over them from his job in this lab hauling boxes of radioactive waste. I thought how his hands would feel like sandpaper sliding over my skin.

He started telling me Deli-King stories, like the time him and Kirk were in there and tried to steal one of the little pictures of the Parthenon off the wall. That was a few years ago.

"You sure've been here a long time—the way everyone knows you and shit," I said.

Then he came as close as I'd ever seen to getting annoyed. He said he was planning to move to New York real soon. He was sick and tired of Boston—he couldn't get any good band going here cause he already knew everybody and he knew he didn't want to play with any of them.

Nothing happened on our date, except that we came up with an idea for a band. I was already just starting as the drummer in a hard-core band called Train Wreck, but I didn't see why I couldn't do a band with

7

Juan too. It was going to be called Elvis: What Happened? I was going to be the Elvis impersonator and Juan would play guitar. We'd do the music that Elvis would have done if only the Colonel hadn't put him in all those corny movies. Juan was sure that if it weren't for the Colonel, Elvis would've gotten together with Jimi Hendrix, so he was going to play his guitar like Jimi would've.

I said to Juan, "This is a good idea and all, but something about it seems weird. I mean, everybody talks about what Elvis would've been like, but I've been thinking that you couldn't have an Elvis without a Colonel Parker. That's just the way it is, you know?" I was kind of kidding, but in another way, I wasn't. I said, "It's like, see, at the cosmic level there's an Elvis force and a Colonel Parker force, and the Elvis force is everything young and cool and the Colonel force is everything old and mean and money-grubbing. But they're two sides of the same thing; they're the same person."

Juan was laughing at me, which made me kind of mad, but then he said, "That'll be part of Elvis: What Happened? We'll start with a dimmed light, and you'll walk out in your Elvis costume and explain that." Maybe that's why Elvis: What Happened? never got off the ground. Right from the beginning it was too conceptual.

Well, actually, the other problem was Juan. He kept playing out of my singing range, so I go, "Come on, you're only playing in B flat. I can't sing that low."

8

He goes, "I can't help playing in B flat. That's my key. I'm just a one-key Portugee."

And every time I fucked up, Juan seemed to take it like a sign that the whole thing would never work out. He'd hunch up over his guitar more and maybe run up and down the scales once, like he was already thinking about something else.

I kept going, "Juan, I know it sounds bad now, but it'll get good if we practice."

This guy in Train Wreck used to play with Juan and he tells me, "Juan's a nice guy, and an amazing guitarist when he was with the Tumors. But he was so depressed when I tried to play with him that I had to drop him." I was wondering if maybe Juan was too good of a guitarist for all of us.

9

ONE DAY WE went to a party at Timmy's. Timmy and her friends are the fashion kind of punk, like with dyed hair that hangs just right over their eyes, antique clothes and pointy English shoes—and always look like they just took a shower.

Me, I'm tall and I was muscular then because I worked at UPS throwing boxes onto the trucks. Plus, I had a crew cut. This particular day, I was wearing what I always wear: combat boots, jeans and a muscle shirt so my tattoo showed.

All the fashion punks were ignoring me. To top it off, Juan was kind of ignoring me too. He was talking to Timmy mostly and I was wondering whether they'd ever slept together. She had on this '60s miniskirt that showed just how toothpicky her legs were. I couldn't take it. I was sick anyways, so I told Juan I was leaving.

I walked home and got in bed—had chills and was lying under all my blankets shivering. I nodded out in that weird way you do when you get a fever, but woke up when I heard Juan come home. I was thinking, "Is he going to come up to my room?" and he did. He stood in the doorway for a minute, looking at me lying there.

"My face is numb," he said. "I can't understand it; I only had two drinks." He walked over to my bed like he was walking in a moving subway car, hands out in front of him. He looked around for a minute like he didn't know what to do, then he sat on my bed, his hip on my stomach through the covers.

I was sure they'd put 'ludes in his punch, the way he could barely stand up a minute ago but could still talk—which is 'ludes, not booze. I didn't want to waste this opportunity of having him wasted, so I go, "Juan, tell me something. How come people are always saying you were different when you were in the Tumors? And how come you guys broke up?"

He said, "I don't know. After a while it wasn't clicking. One day I walked out of practice and didn't come back. When the band broke up, I realized I was just some moron who carts around radioactive waste for a living."

I couldn't understand how he could think he was a failure. I go, "You're the best guitarist in Boston. You could play with any band you wanted. And, besides, what about New York? You're going to move to New York."

"I'll never get there," he said. "I can't even get a band together here."

"What about our band?" I said.

He massaged my shoulder. "Yeah, well, what we're doing is okay, but it's a joke, a joke band."

When he first came into my room, the sun was just setting, and I'd been watching the sky out my window going from reddish to purple. It was getting to be twilight, but I didn't turn on the lamp next to my bed. It looked like the air in my room was turning purple too. I couldn't see Juan's face anymore. He goes, "Spike," and rakes one drunk hand through my crew cut.

Then Juan, just a shadow, lays down next to me.

"Are you crazy?" I said. "I'm sick. You're going to catch my disease."

"I don't care," he says. Then he kisses me. The way he does it is sucks, like he's sucking all the air out of me and my lungs will collapse. But then his hand on my stomach is real gentle, and he's sweet and calls me Priscilla. And soon all the light fades and it's night in my room.

LATER THAT NIGHT I woke up and saw Juan was sitting up in bed with his head leaned against the wall. I thought maybe he was watching me sleep. But when I asked him what he was doing, he said, "Just thinking."

I started thinking how when I was fourteen and didn't even know what punk was, he was hanging out with Meat Hook and all those guys.

11

I sat up beside him. The moon was over the electric plant out my window, and his chest was lit up white, with shadows where his ribs were. I stretched out my arm, twisting it so he could see my tattoo. "Know why I got this?" I said. I told him about the upside-down Jesus. I said, "In my dream he looked like you."

"As handsome as Juan Hombre?" he said.

"I'm serious. Promise me you won't laugh at me?"

"No," he said.

But he didn't really mean it, so I said, "It seems like everybody who's really cool knows this secret. You know it; I can tell you do. I want to know what it is more than anything."

"Spike, that doesn't make any sense. Believe me, if there was a secret I would tell you what it was." But I thought he was just saying that cause I wasn't cool enough to know it: the secret was what Juan knew in that picture where he's screwed up in the air; what Meat Hook knew when they put him in the bin; what Elvis knew, sitting on the can, when his own Jesus touched him on the forehead, right where his third eye would be.

"LOOK IT'S NOW or never," I said, cause I was getting a week off from UPS soon. In a week, I figured, there wasn't time to hitch or even drive. We'd have to fly. I had the money, cause UPS paid good.

"Okay," Juan said. He said okay but I'd have to lend him some cash.

I was fine now—I always get well right away—but Juan was sick as a dog. He was coughing and sneezing and he slept even more than usual. He'd been sick for weeks, but he wouldn't go to the doctor. He wouldn't even take aspirin; all he'd do is pop downers once in a while. It was like he just wanted to lie there and suffer.

But he said he'd go to Graceland anyways. My UPS job was driving me crazy and I felt like if I didn't go somewhere, I'd go insane. Besides, I guess I had some idiot idea that things would be better if we were traveling. We hadn't slept together since that first time, maybe cause Juan was sick. We'd fool around, but then he'd say, "I'm sorry, Spike, I'm tired now."

THIS MIGHT SOUND stupid, but once we were in the airport, he looked different. I mean, nobody recognized him as Juan Hombre, and when I saw him kind of slumped in his airport chair, coughing, looking older even than thirty, for the first time I saw him like he probably saw himself.

Plus, we were on this crappy, cheap airline probably just set up for punks and people like that who don't really give a fuck if they crash.

And Juan, he hadn't even bothered to take Contac or anything. We take off and suddenly he gets quiet, just sitting there with his head in his hands, going, "My ears, oh shit," cause his ears couldn't pop since they were all clogged.

WE GOT TO Graceland by afternoon. They make us line up outside and the fat people with the "It's hard being this sexy, but someone's got to do it" T-shirts are giving me the eye. I tried to tone down my act for

13

Graceland—sneakers instead of combat boots—but I still stuck out way more than in Boston.

This perky Graceland tour girl makes us file through the door all in a line. Juan and me were laughing at her accent cause when she told us to stay with the group it sounded like she was saying for us to stay with the grape.

Inside, in front of every room, was another Barbie-doll zombie tour guide who said stuff and when you walked to the next room you could hear them saying exactly the same thing all over to the next people.

The stairs are right there when you walk in, but we didn't see them at first cause we went with the herd over to the dining room. Then Juan grabbed my arm, going, "Spike, look." The stairs were roped off.

I was pissed, fucking pissed. I went up to one of those Barbie dolls and said, "Are we going to get to go upstairs and see the bathroom where he died?"

"No, I'm sorry, Ma'am," she said.

"This sucks. I can't believe this." I started raving about how pissed off I was, right there in Elvis's living room where he probably did a lot of ranting and raving himself. The difference was at least he got to see the bathroom.

WE DID IT all, every last idiotic Graceland thing—toured the Lisa Marie and the Hound Dog, his airplanes; watched a corny movie called "The Dream Lives On"; took pictures in front of the grave.

When Graceland closed, we sat on the sidewalk of Elvis Presley Boulevard waiting for a bus to come and take us somewhere to sleep—a motel, a park, what-ever. Even though it was six, the heat was still blowing off the highway, blasting us every time a bunch of cars passed.

Not having seen the bathroom, man, I still felt so burned I had to smoke a joint and mellow out. I told Juan he shouldn't cause of his cough but he did anyways.

We were leaning against the wall around Graceland, which had writing all over it. I started walking up and down, reading; each stone had one message to Elvis written on it like "Motor City Hell's Angels Know Elvis Is Still the King," or "Freddie from Alaska came here to see you 3/12/84." I found an empty stone and wrote, "Elvis I came to see the toilet you died on but they wouldn't even let me upstairs."

15

When I sat down again, I noticed Juan had kind of fainted. His head was leaned up against the wall and his eyes were slits.

I hit him on the shoulder. "Come on, Juan, man, you can't sleep here."

He said, "Spike, I feel like shit," which was weird, cause in all the time he'd been sick, he hadn't com-plained once I don't think. He looked all pale under his dark skin, and when he coughed he sounded like an old man in a bus station. I slid my eyes over his way, wondering what the hell I was doing there with him.

It was starting to get dark and he'd fallen asleep leaned against the wall when this purple Pontiac, with fins and everything, pulls up to the gate in front of

Graceland. A black lady gets out and, real businesslike, opens a vial, pouring white powder in a line across the road, right in front of the gate.

I got up and ran over to her. "Excuse me," I said, "do you know when the downtown bus comes by here?"

"Ain't no buses after six o'clock," she said. She had hair all stiff and wavy, like a wig, and was wearing a cotton dress with little flowers on it. She was old, about my mom's age, I guess. She looked at me for a minute, then said, "If you want a ride somewheres, get on in back."

"Wait a sec. Let me get my friend." I went and waked up Juan. He said, "You got us a ride? You're great, Spike," then limped along behind me and we got in the backseat of the car. I was kind of ashamed for her to see me with him, some old sick guy.

She already had the car running, and when we got in, she backed out onto the highway. I said, "If you could just drop us off downtown, like anywhere, that would be great."

"Don't you children want some dinner? Let me fix you some."

I looked at Juan, but he had his eyes closed. I go, "Sure, that would be really nice. Do you live in town?"

She half-turned her face to me, only for a second, but I thought I saw a design of dots on her forehead, darker than her skin. "No, honey. I live way out in the country."

When she said that, it was like one part of me started freaking, imagining all kinds of ax murder scenes in this house of hers. But this other part of me knew it would be okay.

After a while, she turned off the highway. It was dark now, and I could tell we were in the boonies, cause all I saw in the light from her headlights was trees and mailboxes—tin boxes on top of sticks along the road.

Finally, she turned onto a dirt road and parked. We got out and followed her up this hill all covered with weeds and frizzy bushes. On top was her house, which looked like a dark, big box blocking out the stars.

"You live alone?" I said. It kind of occurred to me that she could have a son who would beat us up.

"My husband, Henry, he's over at the Night Owl watching the game on TV. That gets him of my hair once in a while," she said, kind of laughing. The door wasn't even locked. We walked in and it was dark in there and smelled perfumey, like incense. She turned on a lamp and said, "Now you sit here and I'll get us something to eat."

We were in a living room all crammed with weird shit—a big framed picture of JFK with ribbons hanging down from it, baby dolls, Christmas lights, a deer head trophy with designs painted on its fur, a Buddha with a red lightbulb on top of his head, and a hubcap with a crucifix in the middle of it. Juan and me sat down on this couch the color of a tongue. Juan had waked up some and he said, "Looks like home," meaning our house in Boston.

The lady came back with bowls on a tray, and sat down in a chair opposite us. She handed me a bowl and I started eating this hot, spicy stew.

She said, "Now tell me how come you children are down here?"

I told her about Graceland, about how I wanted to see the bathroom where Elvis died cause of my dream about him. She laughed. "I shoulda known." Then she went off on a wild story. She looked at me when she told it, like Juan wasn't there.

"This is a secret," she said, leaning forward. "In the few years before she died, my mamma ministered to Elvis's hairdresser. Mamma was a spiritualist, born with a veil over her face. She lived here with us, and when the hairdresser came for love potions and such, I'd hear all kinds of things, cause he was so fond of talking about Elvis.

"Towards the end, Elvis, he was studying Voodoo. He goes down to Schwabs, the five-and-dime on Beale Street, and buys all of them fake books on Voodoo. He reads all them books and thinks he knows everything, like he's some kind of swami, even took to wearing a turban, I hear.

"Mamma, she tells the hairdresser to warn him; she just knows something bad is waiting to happen to him if he keeps this up.

"A few days later, that hairdresser comes back and what do you think? He says Elvis told him he had a funny dream. He dreamed Jesus was standing over his bed looking at him. This Jesus got a crown of flames and he's holding keys.

"Mamma says, 'That ain't Jesus, that's Pappa Legba, king of the dead. Tell Elvis not to mess with Voodoo anymore. Tell him to stop taking them pills.' By now

18

Elvis wasn't just reading the five-and-dime stuff; he'd got ahold of the real thing—bought it from some bad Voodoo men for near five hundred dollars. Listen, honey, if you go making money off Voodoo, that's black magic you're doing. Likewise if you make a spell that hurt anybody else. Those men, they stand down by the river with the drunks. They sold Elvis a book, spells on how to kill people, how to make folks do what you say.

"And a week later, Elvis died. He was reading a book, the bad Voodoo book. We found out from the hairdresser. And you know what page it was on?"

The lady leaned forward and I leaned forward, even though I thought she was bullshitting me. "What?" I said.

"It was open to a spell—a few words you say, that's all—for summoning up Pappa Legba. Now anybody with sense knows you can't make Pappa Legba do anything; only reason you call him up normally is so you can ask his advice kind of, cause sometimes things here get out of line with the spirit world."

I was playing along, since it was her house and her food. "Don't you wonder what Elvis asked him to do?"

"Yes, I do," she said, real serious. "Elvis must of told him to do something, then Pappa was mad and struck him dead. Or maybe that's what Elvis wanted in the first place—to be dead."

I looked at Juan. He was still eating, his spoon shaking when he held it to his mouth. He smiled at me, even though I don't think he'd been listening to her really. I was hoping the lady didn't notice how out of it he was.

I thought she was trying to fake me out, so I said kind of sarcastically, "How come you're telling us all this? Isn't it a big secret?"

She said, "I thought you should know, since you got the cross of Legba on you."

She was looking at my arm—at my tattoo I realized. "My tattoo is the cross of Legba? Well, then it's just some kind of coincidence, cause I didn't know that when I got it," I said.

She goes, "Ain't no coincidences. You're a child of Legba."

She goes into telling me about him. Says he watches over crossroads and thresholds—that's why the keys. When people die he comes to get them and if you want to talk to spirits, you got to go through Pappa Legba. He's like the bouncer of the spirit world, I guess.

And I had the same feeling I did when I saw the upside-down cross in the bathroom in Boston—like everything was falling into place, and would keep on falling into place.

VIV—THAT WAS her name—said to Juan, "Here, take this pill." She was standing over him and he took it from her and put it in his mouth, before I could say anything. Juan, that guy never thought twice before taking a pill.

He looked up at her leaning over him and goes, "Do you mind if I lie down?"

"Not at all, sweetie, stretch your legs out," she said, and I stood up so he could put his legs where I was sitting. I took off his shoes for him. They were black lace-ups, the leather all cracked and scratched, with a hole on the bottom of each.

She showed me the extra room where Juan and me could stay after she made the bed. Like the rest of the house, this room was just full of stuff. There was an old wood cabinet with glass shelves and through the glass I could see all these amazing things, like a little mosaic bird made out of colored mirrors and something that looked like someone's cut-off hand.

She goes, "This was to be my baby's room, but she died before she was even out of me."

I was afraid to say something wrong, so I kept my mouth shut.

"It's okay," she said, "it was nineteen years ago—I've come to live with it." I was freaking, cause I was nineteen. I wanted real bad to look in that room, but already we were walking down the dark hall to the kitchen, and we ended up sitting in there. She brought us each a glass of lemonade. I started to drink it, but she laughed and said, "Hang on there," and poured something from a flask into each of our glasses.

The kitchen was all dark, and the floor was crooked, which made me kind of seasick. There were plants, herbs I guess, hanging upside-down from the wooden beams in the ceiling.

I ended up telling her practically my whole life story. She listens like she's heard it before. Her dark skin shines blue sometimes and I like that. Every one of her

21

fingers has a ring on it, like Liberace's. While I talked, I heard her breathing in and out the way she breathes.

Sometimes when I say something she goes, "Ummmmm-hmmmmm." When she heard my story, she said, "Most bad children are just bad, but some few are the children of Legba. They're bad cause they've got power gummed up inside them. Never happened to me, cause my mamma knew what to do, how to keep the power running through me. She used to sprinkle dirt from a graveyard on me when I was asleep."

"Geez," I said. "I wish someone'd done that for me, man. My childhood sucked."

Somehow we started talking about Juan. "He's not always such a mess," I said. I told her what he was like when he was in the Tumors.

She goes, "The more power you got, more can go wrong."

I said, "What about your mom? Didn't it go wrong with her?"

She leaned forward, even closer than before. She said, "She knew how to hang onto it. It ain't a secret, it's a science, something you got to follow at every turn and keep learning every day." She sat up straight again. "We women pass that science down one to the other cause you sure can't trust a man with the power. They spend it like money for booze, but we know how to keep it till we're all sucked up and old. Not that I have anything against men. They start out pretty, and when they're past that, they can work and earn you money, like my Henry. But they sure cannot understand about power, honey."

We were still talking an hour or two later when Juan walked in. He said, "I was wondering if you have any Kleenex?"

"There's paper napkins on the shelf there," she said.

"Thanks." He took one and blew his nose until he'd used up the whole napkin. "Thank you for your help. I'm feeling much better." He can be real polite sometimes.

"You ready for bed now?" Viv said.

"Yeah," he said. It was only about ten, and Viv said she was staying up to wait for Henry.

AFTER VIV FINISHED the bed and left the room, I took a look in that glass cabinet. What I thought was a bird made out of colored mirrors turned out to be the edge of a picture frame. I pulled it out: it was a square made of clay with colored mirrors and gold stars and silver moons all stuck in it. Inside the square was a picture of a black girl. It was all old and faded, and the girl was wearing a black dress, which didn't seem like a dress on her cause she was so muscular.

Juan had been sitting on the bed while I looked around. I sat next to him. "The plane leaves tomorrow," I said.

"It's been a great trip, Spike. I'm glad you got us down here." He was always sweet like that, giving me the credit.

"I don't think I'm going to go back right now. Viv said I could stay here."

23

I expected him to freak out, but he said, "I thought maybe you were going to say something like that." He put his arms around my waist and leaned his head on my shoulder. "I always knew you were too cool for Boston. You're so cool, Spike." I guess that in his own lazy, half-assed way he loved me.

"I'm going back," I said, kind of weirded out. "I'm just staying here for a week or something, not forever."

"Yeah, right," he said. "I don't know about that."

And then, by way of saying good-bye, we did it for a long time, real gentle. Later, middle of the night, I wake up and see he's staring at the floor where the moonlight, coming through the window, makes six squares.

"What are you thinking about?" I say.

"What I always think about. I'm trying to figure out where I fucked up." The hollow of his neck has a few beads of sweat in it, like a cup with only the last few drops of a magic potion inside. I lean over him to lick out each one.

24

The Dead Rabbit Pocket

MY FATHER ALWAYS wore the most beau-
tiful clothes when we went riding together. In particular, I remember his hunting coat, which was the color
of dried blood and had a pocket inside for dead rabbits.

He took me to the museum to see the pictures of
horses. The camera had frozen them in mid-gallop.
The pictures were lined up in rows to show how a
horse runs. My father said that before they invented a
fast enough shutter, no one knew that a galloping
horse lifts all its hooves from the ground at once. He
pointed to the frame that proved this point. The horse
didn't look as if it was galloping, with all its hooves in
the air; it looked perfectly still, all spliced up in time
like that.

On my birthday, my father took me to a special
place—not a riding school, but an academy. It was

immaculately clean; I had never seen horses surrounded by such cleanliness. I suppose it was the sort of place where my father must have ridden when he was a child. He looked perfect leaning against the spotless wood in his jodhpurs and boots, his coat.

He said, "Ride any horse you want."

The lady who ran the stable showed me a pony she thought I would like. It was like all the other ponies I had ever ridden: barrel-chested, gentlemanly, wise in its way.

I had already cantered. I had already ridden over the cantilevered bars. It was my ambition that day to gallop.

In the stall next to the pony, a big horse was waving his head around. He was the color of a blue-black bruise.

I said, "I want to ride him."

My father said, "Now that you're ten, I trust you to make decisions. I think in this case we both know what the wise decision is."

I said, "You promised—any horse." I knew I had him. My father was always as good as his word.

They had to lift me onto that horse, he was so tall. My father said he would put a lead line between our horses' bits so that mine couldn't bolt. I felt it was an indignity to be attached to my father by means of this equestrian umbilical cord.

We rode past a paddock and a ring, toward the trail. When my father held out his arm to snap the lead line onto my horse's snaffle, I reined my horse's head away.

I said, "First I'm going to go into the ring. Alone."

I guess my father was too surprised to say anything. He continued to lean toward me, holding out the lead line.

I rode away from him, into the ring. The minute the horse walked through the gate, he yanked his head so that the reins flew from my fingers. He took off in a gallop and I lost my stirrups. The only thing to hold onto was his mane; my hands were my anchors as I bounced high in the air.

The horse galloped around the ring once, past my father, who was yelling something I couldn't hear. I was not as much afraid of falling off as of being stuck forever on that horse, going around and around the ring. If that happened, my father would have to bring me sandwiches and hold them out at arm's length so I could grab them as I went by. My poor father would have to come every day, that long drive.

The next time the horse went around the ring, he headed straight for the stable, oblivious of the fence that stood in his way. In fact, he galloped even faster, if such a thing was possible. He made that *huh, huh, huh* sound. His neck was straight out, like a wooden plank. Right before the fence, he planted his feet and tucked his head in. I rolled along his neck and BAM!

Down on the ground, the horse's hooves were landing around me like bombs. They raised the dust in great puffs. I could see my tiny, faraway father jumping off his horse.

The next instant, he was helping me up, the horse grazing beside us. My father reached into the pocket inside his coat, the pocket in which he used to keep

27

dead rabbits. But all he pulled out was a handkerchief, and all he did was wipe my face.

My father said, "I wanted to help you. I couldn't do anything. I just couldn't do anything. I tried to, but I couldn't do anything." He kept saying things like that.

THAT NIGHT MY father read me a story about elves. They dance inside mushroom circles called "elf rings." If you wander into one of these, you will be trapped inside and the elves will dance you around until you die.

When I went to bed, I noticed a bruise blooming on my hip. It was in the oval shape of the ring in which I had ridden that day. That bruise seemed a mark, a judgment against me.

As I drifted off, I wondered why my father hadn't simply used the camera from the museum to stop the horse. I realized, as I neared sleep, that all I had to do was ask my father to take a picture of me tomorrow, that the camera would stop me from growing up.

It seems to me that I'm always in that ring now, going around and around on that horse that nothing can stop, not the shutter of a camera, not my father. I can see my poor father, who's driven such a long way to help me. He climbs up on the fence and calls instructions I cannot hear. He looks terrified as he leans out holding the sandwich that he has taken from the inside pocket of his blood-red coat, the pocket in which he used to keep dead rabbits.

Stripping

MONTHS AGO, SHE'D written "Henry" on the calendar with the photograph of a covered bridge. Now days had passed and brought her to that square with his name on it, as neat as neat. She had thought of this day as the covered bridge in the calendar picture; she'd seen it from afar, a dark place she would have to pass through. But in more than seventy years, she had never gotten used to the way time passed: one sees things coming, but as to what they'll be like, what's inside that tunnel, one never knows.

He'd be here soon, so she began to lay everything out: the raw sugar, linen napkins, cream, lemon wedges, delicate spoons. Lastly, she opened the cupboard to fetch the best teacups. She was too careful to stack them. Instead, she kept each one separate and upside-down on a piece of flannel. Now, as she reached into the cupboard, it occurred to her that the cups looked like brittle skirts billowing into bells, so that as she turned them over she imagined she'd find girls' legs kicking inside.

She hadn't really known Henry since she was thirteen; he must still think of her as little Nannie. She had a picture of herself then, of a girl standing in front of the farmhouse, dressed up in her sailor suit with the serge skirt. In her thin face, her mouth blooms like a bruise; her eyes are hooded and sleepy; there is a dreamy look about her. This girl, Nannie, loved things deeply—the arch of the draft horse's hooves as they picked their way through the mud; her mother's song that started "Speed bonny boy like a bird on the wing"; the buttery smell of her own house when she came back from school. That girl had her violent tempers, too; she'd run away once in the morning, and had only come back when the sky turned as dark blue as a milk of magnesia bottle.

She hadn't seen Henry much since that bad business so long ago; certainly they'd never talked of it. He'd moved to North Carolina, married a girl down there. But he would have heard how she'd grown tall and spindly; how she wore precarious wire-rimmed glasses to read; how she went to teachers college and graduated at the top of the class; how her mouth had wilted into a grim line.

She had a picture from college, too. She was seated amid the rows of women in white, a group like a flock of birds about to fly off and scatter to all parts of the country with the mission of drilling grammar and mathematics into lazy heads.

In the last years before she retired, she taught by rote, droning rules about commas and semicolons to students who wouldn't listen anyway. But in the beginning, teaching had been a battle; she'd had something dreadfully important to impart to those seventh graders who sat before her. "We may die, but Shakespeare doesn't; that is why literature is such a comfort," she'd say, though it was only an approximation of what she meant. When spring came, and the smell of new-mown grass filled the classroom, she gave them extra homework. Books, how she loved books! She wanted her seventh graders to love them too, instead of wallowing in the great green spring of adolescence, that dreamy sadness that had caused her so much pain.

31

She married a history teacher, but it didn't last three years. Henry would have heard of that; he might have speculated along with the rest of them, might even have come close to guessing what went wrong.

She hadn't known it herself until her husband said one day, "Nan, at first I thought you were shy, but now I know you have a wall up." He pronounced this like a man who'd already made his decision, those solemn blue eyes boring into her. She preferred it when he wore his glasses rather than when he stared at her with those naked eyes, fringed by pale-blond, almost-invisible lashes. Until he'd said this, she honestly had no idea that people lived other than with their own separate thoughts spun like cottony cocoons around them. She hadn't known that he'd want her to strip everything away, to let him see not just the broad and proper cloth of her thoughts, but all the Victorian frippery and fribble, all that was her own and no one else's.

Oh, but he always wanted something! If she tried to get a moment's peace, his thin, querulous voice would call from somewhere in the house, "Nan? Nan? What are you doing?" Soon, whenever he talked she heard that peevish whine, as if everything he said was really, "Nan? Nan? What are you doing?"

They never argued exactly, but suffered through an icy politeness until they decided to part. She'd gone back to teaching, to her majestic order and calm; she liked that. In her forties, there had been another man, the owner of the bakery down the street, a widower; Sunday was their day together, for years, but she wouldn't marry him. "Not that again," she'd said, meaning that she liked to go where she pleased and do as she wanted, even if it was lonely sometimes. Living in her own apartment was like waking up each morning to fresh-fallen snow on the street outside, everything dazzlingly white and unspoiled.

But lately—in the last ten years—people had started dying: her mother and father, one of her brothers, her ex-husband, childhood friends. In death, they became not the old people she last knew, but a kind of pure essence of themselves, a knot of memories that defied chronological time. Her mother, for instance, she remembered as a breathtakingly young woman, her lips pursed to hold hemming needles; at the same time, she was a voice singing about the bonny boy and a withered woman stepping over a puddle in a city street, the farm sold long ago. Her brother she remembered as sound, the rustling and laughing behind her as he chased her through the field where the silver tassels on the corn stuck up like wild hair; he was also a stiff, uniformed man in a picture on a long-ago mantle.

As each one died and reverted to a person from her childhood, she felt as if she were herself becoming young Nannie again. She was no longer afraid to take the hands of her friends, her sisters, her grandnieces and nephews, to say, "You are such a joy to me! How much I love you and think about you!" so they smiled back and her eyes brimmed with tears as they always had when she was a girl. Even the madness came back; she had sudden urges to sweep every piece of porcelain off her mantel, and at these times she called her sister Maisie and they had long, petulant quarrels about sewing stitches and tea cakes and who lost whose doll and what year it had been.

At better times, she surprised Maisie with the minute details she remembered from their girlhood together; lately, her memories had become so vivid to be almost a burden. Oh, the clover taste of the fresh milk that left a white ghost of fat on her glass!

And then, several months ago, she'd been on the bus and a young man with a cruel set to his jaw sat down beside her. He was the very image of her cousin Jason. The warmth coming off him and his delicate, hand-some face terrified her. She'd had nightmares like this as a girl—Jason would appear out of nowhere, and

33

when she tried to tell her parents, tried to form a sentence, there was something like cotton stuffed in her mouth.

She'd never told anyone what he'd done. At the time, she hadn't known how to describe it to her parents, or even if it had been her fault. But there on the bus, after almost sixty years, the cotton came out of her mouth. The word for what had happened sat on her tongue. She had to tell it—the word—to someone and the someone she decided on was Henry.

WHEN SHE WAS thirteen, she was sent to stay with her uncle and aunt; they'd had seven children, though only two were left at home. Henry was her age, and only a few inches taller than she. He had sagging shoulders and a slow way of looking over at you, as if he were putting off having to meet your eyes.

But Jason, what a handsome boy he'd been that summer—seventeen or eighteen, tall, with an almost feminine beauty to his face. When he got laughing, he'd go on longer than the joke was funny, convulsing, almost crying. She and Henry would keep tittering along with him, but in the end, their laughter belonged to Jason. That's how it was when you were with him—he had the ideas, he told you what to do.

At first, she thought that when he called Henry "Runt" it was out of teasing affection, that the brothers were close. But one day Jason drank some juice that turned his lips dark, and Henry said, "Hey, it looks like you have lipstick on." Jason jumped on Henry and bent his arm backwards. The position seemed like a

34

familiar one for the boys, and when Jason finally hurled down his brother's arm it was as if he'd beaten up Henry so many times that it had become boring. After that, she'd understood that you just didn't cross Jason, and that even at the best of times Henry was straining to stay on his good side.

Mostly Jason ignored her, though Nannie suspected that, when he tossed sack after sack of feed off the wagon without stopping to rest, he did it for her. His voice was loud and his gestures exaggerated, as if he knew he was being admired.

Henry never did say anything about Jason, until she asked him straight out, on the morning of the very day it happened. They'd gone walking, and after a mile or so had stopped to rest on a rock deep in the woods. She knew it was safe to talk there—they would have heard Jason coming from far off because of the rustle of the ferns and jewel weed and crow's foot.

She carefully tore a leaf in half. "You must hate the way Jason bullies you," she said, and then, after it was out of her mouth, wished she hadn't. There was something about Jason that made her sure he'd hear whatever she said; no matter where you hid, there was no way to cross him and get away with it.

"I wish he were dead," Henry burst out, slapping the rock beside him. A branch above them jumped, the leaves whipping. Henry hunched down with his face against his knees. Then they heard the crow caw and the flutter of wings as it flew away.

"Sweet Jesus," Henry said. "You see how it is? I'm always terrified. You don't know what I've been through—how mean he can be. You haven't seen him."

"We should teach him a lesson," she said.

"What can *we* do to him?"

"Well," she said, "we can just ignore him, that's all. How will he feel when no one pays any attention to him?"

But the strange thing was, that afternoon they walked down to the swampy part of the river, to the old cow shed where they knew they'd find Jason. Maybe it was just that they'd grown bored with each other during that long afternoon, and anything was better than boredom on a worn-down farm in the scrubby part of Tennessee.

Jason was working on a broken gear box; he'd set it on one of the mildewy bales of hay out in front of the shed. His shirt was off, and when he polished rust off the metal, the muscles in his arms and the tendons in his neck stood out. As they waded toward him through the wild wheat grass, he looked up and smiled. "I'm hot as an old goat," he called. "We should take a swim."

Nannie felt her face splitting into a smile. There was nothing better than Jason in a good mood; she'd almost forgotten that.

"Hey," Jason said, and bent to pick up what she thought was a rock. "Look at this." He chucked it against the wall of the shed and it exploded—a dried-out cow pie. He threw one at Henry, and suddenly the three of them were running in a wild circle throwing cow pies at each other, laughing until they could barely breath; after a few minutes, they moved into the shed, rooting through the soggy hay for more.

And then in the midst of their frenzy, she reached down and time seemed to stop when she touched the treasure: a glob of manure still moist as dough, big as a breadloaf. She scooped it into her arms, straw and all, and looked up; they were snorting with laughter, both of them, watching to see who she'd throw it at. And in that moment she made a choice for which she'd always blamed herself; she pretended to heave it at Henry, but at the last minute she twisted so that the cow pie hit Jason right in the chest, splattered across his bare skin, and pricked his shoulders and face with black moles. She hadn't meant to aim so well. She began to laugh, a harsh barking sound, and then stopped herself.

Jason wiped some of it off his face. Everything went quiet as he narrowed his eyes down to slits. She and Henry froze, waiting. She felt how her pulse beat in her ears, and smelled the machine oil and the sickly sweet of the cow dung in the heat.

"Runt," Jason said, "look how she's split the side of her dress so you can see right in." Nannie reached down and saw it was true: her thin, threadbare summer dress gaped away from one side of her body, right below the waist. She pinched it closed.

When she looked up, their faces were all in a shine but no smiles; she understood then that Henry had gone to his brother's side.

"I can't help it," she said.

Jason drew nearer, more than a head taller than she was, skin gummed with sweat, splatted with black. "I

37

saw," he said. He looked over her shoulder at Henry and said, "Runt, take off the dress."

At that moment, she should have run; but the truth was, as much as it terrified her to have his slitted eyes go up and down her body, she was thrilled at the delicious dirtiness of it. All summer she'd watched him; all summer she'd waited for him to look at her like that.

She felt Henry's hands, birdlike, gentle, at her back.

"Step out of it," Jason said to her, and staring at him, hypnotized, she stepped out of her dress.

"Her underthings, Runt," Jason said.

Then she stood naked as an ear of white corn when it's husked too young, all the kernels like tiny, soft pearls. She waited for his eyes to caress her pale breasts with the blue veins running beneath the skin, for him to admire the ripple of her hips. But instead he shook his head, as if he wanted to laugh, and let out a snort of disgust; then she knew how her nakedness really looked: sickly and sweaty and ugly as sin, a boy's body gone wrong.

He grabbed her arm.

"What are you doing?" she said, for she hadn't expected anything but for him to look.

Without answering, he put one foot behind her ankle and pulled on her arm so she lost her balance and crumpled in the dirty hay. He held her down with one hand and with the other he undid his pants, as if he were peeing out in the woods. When he slid on top of her, she saw the hollows of his neck, the tendons standing out, and it seemed to her that his whole body was cruel.

"YOU LOOK VERY well," Henry said, as they touched cheeks at the door.

"So do you," she said, though he looked worn out, done in—a little old man gazing up at her with a walnut face. He was so hunched, stooped and battered that his light-blue summer suit wrinkled everywhere, making him look like a balled-up tissue. Her stomach clutched at the thought that this was the same Henry from then; this was the hollow-chested boy who had watched it happen, maybe breathing like a dreamer, mouth open.

She ushered him into the dining room and sat him down. "You must be exhausted. Tea?"

"Thank you," he said, crossing one leg against the other the way a woman does. He looked so undone from the June heat in his mussed collar and college tie that she felt a stab of remorse. Here she was calling him away from his granddaughter, whose graduation he'd come up to see.

But smiling, she placed a cup and saucer, the wedges of lemon, the raw sugar, the pitcher of cream, the spoons and napkins before him. Then she began to chuckle—and in the same reluctant way as when he was a boy, he looked over at her.

"What is it?" he said.

"I suddenly realized how complicated it is to drink a cup of tea," she said. "Look at this artillery of things we have here before us." She meant something else, of

39

course. It seemed to her that each pleasant plate she laid before him was a trap, that she'd made a magic circle around him.

He laughed politely. "I do appreciate your effort." He waved a shaky hand to take in all the crockery, the gleaming silver.

"Oh, no, no, it's a treat for me. You're so kind to come." She bent to pour a golden, steaming stream of tea into his cup. Suddenly, she was aware of him watching and feeling sorry for her, of him thinking how she must be lonely, the way she paid so much attention to the tip of the teapot so the liquid arched perfectly. She shook her head to try to clear away this image of herself, remembering again her true self, as familiar and comfortable in her mind as a chestnut is in the hand. She was the girl he'd followed around all summer; she was young Nannie, the one who ran away from home into the beyond of falling-down fences and secret trails through tall grass.

It was only this image of herself that gave her the courage to sit back down, look him in the eye, and say, "I've been thinking about Jason."

He laughed softly. "Ah, old Jason."

She could tell that he remembered Jason the way they all did—a shadow from long ago, a war hero. She'd seen the bundle of letters with sections blacked out, the photo of a boy in a flight jacket smoking a cigarette, the green velvet ribbon. That was all they had left of him after his plane was shot down over the sea.

"Cream?" she said.

He gazed up. "No, no. My heart."

"You see, he's come to mind," she said, "because something very important happened that summer when I stayed at your parents' house." She tried to sound calm, but she couldn't keep her voice from getting thin and high. Her stomach had gone sour with dread. "I believe you were there," she added.

He blinked several times, then began to laugh. His laugh was low and mellow, the wisest thing about him. "I'm afraid I don't know what you're talking about."

"It's very awkward," she said. She realized she was compulsively smoothing her napkin beside her cup and forced herself to put her hands in her lap. "I'm afraid it's rather awkward," she said again.

He leaned forward a bit, one splayed hand on his trouser knee. "I don't understand, Nannie." He had a condescending air about him—oh, he'd picked up a lot since his scrawny days.

She squinted at him. "You really don't know?" It was all coming back to her now, with him here—even the part she had refused to think about before. She wanted to say "rape." She wanted to use that one word to describe how she'd changed from a sentimental girl into the bitter young woman they all called brilliant. But, to be honest, it was far more complicated than one word, that single syllable, could indicate.

The day it happened, after she and Henry sat on a stone in the woods and made a pact to ignore Jason, they had gone back to the house; they'd sat on the porch playing some stupid game, until finally she'd burst out, "I'm so bored. Let's go down to the river!"

41

He'd complained, of course, that she'd just promised not to. He had stood up and walked to the edge of the porch, his father's land spread out behind him, the white grass blinding in the hard light.

She'd been desperate to go down there. She longed to see Jason's anger, Henry's humiliation, any kind of emotion to break the boredom, the way one craves a thunderstorm to break the heat.

On a whim, she had crept up behind Henry—who was looking off at the glint of river—and grabbed him by his bony shoulders.

She'd felt him stiffen, trying not to move, as if her hands were two birds that might fly off.

"What?" he'd said.

She'd guided him down the steps, laughing at her discovery, at how easy it was to make him do whatever she wanted. "Come on," she'd said and propelled him through the wild wheat grass, the two of them making a path of shiny, bent-down stalks while the cicadas screeched all around them with the beat of someone panting.

He had plodded ahead of her, complaining. "Nannie, quit it. This is stupid." But he hadn't struggled to get free: such were the secret aches of that summer that she'd known he'd put up with anything to keep her hands cupped on his shoulders.

During that walk, it had seemed to her that for the rest of her life she'd lead men from behind, toward whatever destination she wanted. She would be like one of the cruel women in the Bible, Salome or Jezebel, who ruin men's lives with their beauty. Yes, a whole life of sin stretched before her like a delicious meal. That was why she'd been unafraid to throw the cow pie at Jason, and why she'd stripped naked for him.

Now, some small rustle interrupted her thoughts. It was Henry, shifting in his chair. She realized she'd left him waiting for her to speak. When she'd invited him, she had wanted to say, "Jason raped me," and make Henry see he was partly to blame that she'd come to this—a lonely old woman. But no, she liked her life; she had so many friends, so many she loved, though some were dead. She had wanted to say "rape," but now with Henry in front of her, she wanted just as badly to deny it.

After all, she was the girl who let Henry slide her underthings down her legs, his fingers lingering on the smooth skin of her hips. She was the girl who stood whitely naked in the dark of the barn, believing for one moment that the beauty of the hollows under her arms, her thighs like tallow candles, would change Jason into the tenderest boy; believing that her body held a power like light, like the rays that burst around the saints' heads and the heat that turned the corn plump in the summer.

She wanted to say all this, draw the whole scene for him, but what came out was a few, faltering sentences. "It was in the cow shed. My dress ripped and Jason got carried away, and, well . . ." Her voice became breathy and then just ran out.

For a long moment, he said nothing. A truck passed

43

with a rumble, shaking the window pane. "What?" he said coldly. "What are you talking about?"

"We were throwing cow pies. You were there, too. We were playing and then suddenly everything got out of hand." She couldn't control her own voice—she kept gasping between the words—and she thought, quite rationally, This is what happens when people get hysterical.

Something in Henry seemed to settle. Maybe it was the sight of her so undone. He turned from her, his skin looking bluish and brittle in the light from the window. "Oh," he said. "I'd forgotten."

She knew she had him; she felt as if once again her hands were on his shoulders and she was leading him where he did not want to go. "But you remember now?"

"Yes," he said, "what he did to you was terrible." Henry looked at her straight on. "And I didn't help you, did I?"

"That's not what I meant. I didn't mean to blame you. You were scared too."

He studied the little spoon he'd been holding, shaking his head. "Oh Lord," his voice cracked. "You're right. I was so scared of him. That's why I ran away instead of helping you. I was terrified." He stopped, as if that were the end of the story.

"You ran away?" she said. Somehow she'd thought he'd remember it just as she did.

"Yes," he said, his voice measured and melancholy. "I saw him . . . doing that to you and I just bolted."

"That's not what I'm saying. It's just that you were

there and I wanted someone else to remember, too," she said, her voice sounding shrill. "It doesn't matter."

He gripped the table, leaned forward. "It does matter, don't you see? You know, when I was seventeen, I went down to the recruiting office to sign up, but I couldn't even hold the pen because of the way my hand was shaking. So I never went to war and people called me a coward. What I'm trying to say is, when Jason did that to you, it was just the same. I should have helped you, but something inside me crumbled."

Their eyes met. She awkwardly reached over and patted his shoulder. "You were just a boy."

He'd gotten it all turned around, she realized; he remembered it like a moral from one of their old lesson books, as if he'd stood in that barn weighing right and wrong while Jason ripped her clothes off. But the truth was, it hadn't been a bit like a lesson book. Henry had run his finger along the dimple at the small of her back, and—until Jason shoved her down—she'd enjoyed those two boys' eyes on her like the most delicious, ticklish strokes of a feather.

"You," he said, looking at her as if he'd just recognized her. "You've led a hard life. Oh, Nannie, you were a beautiful girl." His voice caught, as if he might cry at the sadness of her. "And I didn't do anything to stop it."

"Henry, please. You've got it all mixed up. It wasn't your fault. It was me; I took my own clothes off for him." She was lying, but in a way it was truer than what really happened. "I was a wild little thing. And when I die, I don't want them to tuck a sheet over me

45

like making a clean bed and think that I never had my sins."

She'd been staring out the window as she talked, at the way the sun through the trees made sequins of light on the street. Now she could hear him breathing loudly, as he had in the barn. When she turned toward him, he had his mouth open and his forehead tight in concentration.

"To tell you the truth, I forgot what happened in the barn because it was one of those Jason memories," he said. "I tried to forget everything he did to me. Don't dwell on the bad, that's my motto. After he died, I tried to think of the positive. But the truth is, he was off his rocker." Henry cleared his throat. For a moment, she thought he'd finished, but he started up again. "By the time you came that summer, he'd made me do a lot of things I don't care to mention."

"Yes," she tried to soothe him with her voice. "You were frightened. You had to run away," she said, though she remembered him standing and watching it all to the end.

"When you came to our farm," his voice cracked with the confession, "you seemed just like Jason. You two would always make jokes I didn't understand. The real truth of the matter is it never crossed my mind to try to save you from him—you'd have laughed at me."

"Yes," she said, "I probably would have."

"And in that barn," he said, gazing off at something behind her shoulder, "I guess I hoped the two of you would just do each other in. The whole thing, the stink, the sounds. I burst out of there, running along the river, and thought how clean the light was on the water, and how I must pray to our Lord Jesus Christ. And, Nannie, you turned to the Lord, too, didn't you? I always assumed that because of how you grew up so decent."

She swiveled to see what he'd been staring at, and it was the calendar hanging on the kitchen door. He'd been speaking to the photograph of the covered bridge instead of her, as if it were a picture of the old cow barn, as if right now their young selves were inside that dun-colored shack.

"No, I just knew how to take care of myself. Jason didn't do any real damage, of course," she said, regaining the haughty tone she'd often used as a child. "I fought him off the way a girl knows how. A girl knows where to kick and how to scratch."

And Henry, hollow-chested as ever, listened as solemnly as that day in the woods when they made a pact between them. She lied on and on, turning Jason into a frail stick figure and herself into a harpy, a hungry hag from a dream; in that barn she had rushed around Jason like a wind, she crushed him to a nub.

"I tempted him like Potiphar's wife, like Delilah, like Eve." As she chanted the names of the evil women, she felt how the delicate shells of tea cups, the picture frames, the porcelain knickknacks hung around her like confining clothes. And she thought how soon, when the end came, all these things would be stripped away from her, until she was as bare and white as that girl in the barn, not innocent now but hard and smoothed down to nothing as a pearl.

47

Shrinks

A FEW MONTHS ago, Sara's mother started taking Prozac. Every Sunday now, she called with more proof of her indebtedness to the drug. "I've quit my job, honey. I'm starting a catering company," she said breathlessly one day, as if she had that minute run in from giving notice. Then, a few weeks later, "I've thrown out my entire wardrobe. I'm only going to wear happy clothes."

Once in a while Sara couldn't help saying something snide like, "What's next, Mom, a tummy tuck?" After all, this happiness of her mother's was a betrayal of sorts.

"Oh, Sara," her mother would say, "give it a rest." Or more likely, she'd advise Sara to stop seeing her feminist therapist and go to someone with an MD:

Her mother had no use for shrinks who couldn't dispense pills.

RIDING THE TRAIN downtown to meet her mother, Sara tried not to catch glimpses of herself in the window, which had been turned by the darkness outside into a black mirror. She thought, "At least I've had more than her," meaning shrinks. Back before the Prozac, she and her mother had spent an afternoon on the phone counting them. Her mother had an amazing memory for shrinks. "You started at seven with that Dr. Prescott. I didn't start until I was sixteen," she'd said, as if excusing herself for her low score. At the end of tallying Sara's shrinks, they'd realized she'd had almost thirty, if you included the counselors at school, the doctors she'd decided against after seeing them once and the ones she'd gone to just to get this or that medicine.

"Very impressive, Sara," her mother had said, in the same stiff way she used to congratulate her after a piano recital.

"Anyone could do it, Mom."

"No, hon, it shows how serious you are about solving your problems. I'm proud of you."

Sara understood what she was really referring to. Her mother had always believed that when she found the right man, the right job, the right pill, her life would begin again. Her mother hadn't considered herself properly alive since Sara's father left her seventeen years ago.

Back before that happened, Sara had only dabbled in psychiatry: the summer she was seven, her mother made matching daisy-print dresses for Sara and herself, and a few days later announced, "You're going to see a psychiatrist just like Mommy." Sara always associated her first session with the terry-cloth pinafore that matched her mom's, with feeling like a little lady as she waited by herself in the reception room, reading *Highlights* the way her mother read the *New Yorker*. All she could remember about her first psychiatrist was the way he asked her about dreams she couldn't remember, and his toys, her favorite of which was the pretend doctor's kit. Inside was a vial of candy pills. "Go ahead," he'd say, "eat one." No matter how many candy pills she ate, the vial was always full again by the next session.

Her mother gave her real pills, too: purple ones for going to sleep; a yellow one to ease her through the first day of third grade; a white one when she got too excited about riding the bumper cars at Playland.

51

After her father left, when Sara was ten, she switched shrinks and began going twice a week. The new psychiatrist didn't have any toys, only a desk, a reclining couch and a box of Kleenex.

"What's the bed for?" she asked him in the first session.

"In case you feel like lying down," he said.

"But why would I feel like lying down?"

"You might; try it," he said.

She tried to lie stiff on her back, but she couldn't keep still; she rolled to her stomach, to her side.

"You don't have to," he said. "It's not necessary."

"Yes it is," she said. Finally, she settled on her back

with her hands on her stomach. She knew that her mother must lie in the same position when she had therapy, carefully resting her perfect bonnet of hair on the pillow.

"Tell me about your father," the shrink's voice had said. She couldn't see him from where she lay; instead she spoke to his framed diplomas, which hung on the opposite wall.

"Daddy's moved to California," she said.

"How do you feel about that?"

"I don't know."

But after several more years of therapy, she knew exactly what she felt, or what she was supposed to feel. Even when she'd graduated to other worries, the shrinks kept dredging up the divorce, and she dutifully went over it with them, giving them what she later realized was her mother's version of the story: without warning or provocation, her father said he couldn't live with them anymore and announced he'd taken a job on the West Coast. Sara, the shrinks said, felt rejected.

Sara sometimes suspected that she was no more unhappy than any of her high school friends. But her mother said, "Sara, normal people jump out of bed in the morning with a smile. We have to fix whatever's making you so depressed." Her mother, in fact, had been through vials of pills searching for the ingredient she thought made other people so happy; she hadn't found it, but she had hopes for Sara, and would drop her off at the shrink's office saying, "Now, honey, if he prescribes you Premerin, make sure you get some Desaril with it so you can sleep," or "Sara, don't let him give you Ellivil. We don't want you to bloat up, do we?"

During college, Sara began going to a feminist social worker instead of a psychiatrist. With her new shrink, she revised the family story: perhaps her mother, brainwashed by the patriarchy, sought to mold Sara into a perfect, plastic girl with no problems. Since that breakthrough, she'd gone to a string of feminists.

Nowadays, Sara was seeing Tillie, a short, squat grandmother who wore serapes she'd woven herself. On her wall, bigger than any of her university degrees, was a blown-up newspaper photo of herself twenty years ago, sprawled in the street, with police officers leaning over her. That she had once laid her body down in front of trucks carrying boys off to Vietnam—or rather, off to an army base in New Jersey—was somehow one of Tillie's credentials for therapy. She valued Life.

53

"Honey," she'd say, "you've been telling me over and over again that you want to quit your job. Now let's discuss how you're going to do that."

But even discussing it made Sara queasy. For four years, she'd worked in a library filing the bound periodicals. She couldn't imagine anything else but days filled with the particular squeak of the floor in the stacks, of watching the dust swirl like fruit flies when she opened an old almanac.

She'd never had a real job in an office, but she'd seen it on TV—people rushing around in suits, phones ringing, the glare of fluorescent lights. Going to work in such a place would be like having to wake up from her dreaming days of shuffling between the iron shelves, trailing one hand along their lines of book spines.

"I'm just too neurotic right now to even think about it," Sara would say.

"What about your boyfriend?" Tillie would remind her. "You say the relationship's going nowhere."

If Sara's job could have been turned into a man—as frogs are turned into princes—it would have been her boyfriend, Andy. He had the musty, outmoded air of the library about him, the way he kept his blinds drawn all day, reading under a sickly circle of light. Sara had dropped out of grad school after a year, but he was the type who would be in it forever. He even looked like a sloth, with his furry sweaters and one lock of hair that hung over his eyes.

"But what if I never get a boyfriend again?" Sara would say. "What if I die alone?"

Tillie would lean forward and wave a hand emphatically, as if trying to erase a chalk board. "You just need a Cause in your life. Something outside of yourself."

All the feminist shrinks said she needed something like that. It was the one point on which they seemed to agree with her mother: Sara was missing some crucial ingredient in her life. When she found it, she would begin a new, happy existence full of meaning, love and light.

AFTER THAT DAY when she and her mother had counted them up on the phone, Sara couldn't stop thinking about her thirty shrinks; she was not yet thirty years old, so it averaged out to more than one a year, which seemed like some kind of accomplishment. The next time her mother called, Sara said, "How long's a football field? I bet if you put them all end to end, all the shrinks I've had, there'd almost be enough for a line across a football field—thirty times five-and-a-half feet, right?" And she went on and did the math.

"You've always loved numbers," her mother said. "If only you could put that to use."

But Sara hadn't been listening. She'd been imagining the shrinks lying end-to-end across the field. She kept on thinking about them for a long time after. When she was supposed to be working, for instance, a random word on a book spine would remind her of the shrinks, and with a little glow of pride she'd remember them. At first she pictured them in a typical football stadium with lime markings and raspy Astroturf, the vast arena lit up by spotlights as if for a nighttime game. But later she refined the image to make it more comforting: she got rid of the football field and imagined instead an abandoned meadow she used to play in as a kid. As she made the shrinks lie head to toe across the meadow, she took stock of them—the ones still living and the dead ones; the child psychiatrists; the Freudians, Rogerians and feminists; the ones who dressed like doctors and the ones who dressed like golfers; the ones who blamed everything on her dysfunctional family and the silent ones. They reclined on their backs in the ticklish, unmown grass in the late afternoon, as swallows swooped and called in the pink sky. In particular, she treasured the quiet of the

55

scene—no sound except the tremulous, surprising flutter of birds as they dipped into the field to catch one last insect. She didn't have to explain anything, to talk and cry and answer questions for those shrinks in the meadow. Instead, she stood on the hill above them, watching how the smoke from their pipes and cigarettes wafted up in lacy puffs to turn gold in the evening light, like the fleecy clouds of eighteenth-century paintings.

Best of all was how, in the tall grass, the line of shrinks would look like a path that led somewhere, a secret road made of rumpled tweed and crossed arms and faces puckered in meditative consideration of her own problems. She liked to think the shrinks blurred into a taut line, an umbilical cord that would pull her along into her new, perfect life.

SARA HURRIED OUT into the six-o'clock darkness. People trotted past her, their scarves waving from their necks like frantic arms. She crossed the street and saw her mother inside Ciao, reading the menu. In the brightly lit restaurant, her mother looked like a mannequin in a store window—skin pale as moonlight but hard as plastic.

It was the first time Sara had seen her since the Prozac, and her stomach tightened. When she opened the door to the restaurant, her mother turned and, with a distracted, exuberant look, came over to kiss her. A bit of the bright-colored silk around her mother's neck floated into Sara's mouth. For a moment, with her mother clutching her, she had a feeling of panic. It seemed to her that, in stepping into the restaurant, she had stepped into a strange country. With its sprays of forsythia and fragile, trembling circles of candlelight, the restaurant seemed part of the beautiful world of her mother's new life.

Her mother pulled back. "I'm exhausted," she said. "I can't wait to sit down." This made Sara feel much better; even if it was only aching feet, her mother still knew pain.

"You look nice. I think you've lost weight," Sara said.

"Don't laugh, but I do Jane Fonda."

Sara didn't know how to answer, now that sarcastic comments were ruled out. Her mother B.P., before Prozac, would say that exercise was a crock; but now she gushed on about how she loved it, and Sara was reduced to polite clichés.

57

As they settled at their table, her mother talked of the client she had landed that day, and of star fruit and mint leaves, which she referred to as her company's signature garnishes. Sara half-listened, marveling at how her mother had redone herself. She used to wear droopy sweater dresses; she used to be one of those gray-complected women you see everywhere in buses and grocery stores.

Her mother had always had it in her though; Sara could see it now in the way she had ordered their lives, had risen so quickly from secretary to office manager. Even depressed, her mother had grit. Sara, on the other hand, would never have grit. She wanted to tell her mother this, to say, "Look, for me maybe there is no great happiness," but she knew this would not sway her mother, or more specifically that the Prozac coursing through her mother's bloodstream made her deaf to common sense.

Her mother led the conversation expertly—as she must do with her clients now—so that just as they began sipping their decaf, she got down to business. "You know, your cousin Beanie's husband practices up here. I want you to go see him, hon. He'll fix you up. If you're not covered, I'll pay for whatever it takes to get you prescribed. I really think he's the one to help you."

Sara agreed to go. After all, her mother had always said she'd slough off her depression once she found the right pill, and she had. Perhaps Prozac would give Sara the courage to go back to grad school, to ditch Andy. Still, she had a doomed feeling about the whole thing; even if she did take Prozac, surely her lack of grit, her attitude problem, would prevent it from working, as if Prozac were some sort of impartial judge that only gave you the happiness you deserved.

Sara's mother turned over her business card and scrawled the name and number on it. And after her mother rushed off to catch a plane, Sara was left on the sidewalk in front of the restaurant, clutching this white square bearing her mother's scribbles, like a prescription written on stiff paper.

ANDY OPENED THE door and she walked in past him, dumping her bag on the sofa.

"Mom's going to get me Prozac," she said as she

took off her coat and draped it over his roommate's bike.

He trailed after her as she hurried through the apartment turning on lights, the radio, the fan. She always did this, even during day. When they'd first started going out, he'd objected—he hated wasting the energy—but after a few months, he'd grown used to it.

"I thought you didn't want the Prozac," he said.

"I may as well try it. You should see what it's done for her."

"But Sara," he said. "Isn't this backsliding? I mean, letting her tell you what pills to take like when you were a kid?"

"This one works, though. I have the same genetics she does, so maybe it will help me, too." She laughed, "Though actually, I doubt it. I'm beyond hope." She headed to the kitchen, to get the pantry light.

She claimed to turn on the lights and radio to scare off burglars. That's how she'd put it, "burglars," as if she were a little kid. Later, when he'd asked her about it again, she'd said, "Okay, I'll tell you the real reason. Because I think it will keep me distracted, which is better than being neurotic," and then she'd giggled.

But lately, he'd begun to realize she had quite a different reason for turning on the lights and for all her other rigid rituals, like the way she insisted on boiling canned food to kill botulism, and her habit of constantly referring to her neuroses as if they were old friends. "What's this mole on my arm?" she'd say, and then, "God, I'm such a hypochondriac." She wasn't much more screwed up than the next person, he

59

thought, but she'd been in psychoanalysis so long that she'd learned to magnify every fear, instead of letting it pass. She was, he'd come to realize, like a person whose wounds never get a chance to heal because she can't stop picking at the scabs.

Sara went out to the kitchen and opened the refrigerator.

"Are you hungry?" he asked.

"No, my mother stuffed me. I just want to see what you have." After a minute, she let the fridge close with a smack.

"I'm just worried about this Prozac thing," he said. "I mean, does it really help or is it like Valium?" He heard that whiny tone come into his voice, as it always did when he tried to get her to think rationally.

"I don't care what it does. I just want it," she laughed nervously.

"But I'm worried that this will make you worse in the end. I mean, what about that article in *Newsweek*?"

"Oh, Andy," she said, "that article was hype. Don't worry so much." And then she laughed, and he started laughing, too, at her telling him not to worry.

DR. MANNING'S OFFICE was in a turreted and long-lawned mansion, the kind of mental hospital that looks like a prep school. She knew the type. The reception area was furnished in that tasteful way— mahogany tables and Liberty prints—that meant one thing to her: liberally prescribed drugs.

"Go right on up," the receptionist said.

But just outside the doctor's office, a rotund, rumpled man motioned to her from down the hall. "Come here," he called. "Over here."

Sara pointed to the office, but he kept waving for her to follow him. "I have an appointment," she said when she caught up.

"It's all right," he said. "That's my office." As she followed him along the hall, he added, "The Xerox machine is broken and I have to copy these forms. I'm very absent-minded, you see, so if I don't do these now, I never will." He led her into a room where a copy machine was still beeping.

"There," he said, pushing the green button for emphasis. "It says E5. E5!"

Sara, who was always fixing the machine at work, said, "That means it needs toner."

The doctor turned in a circle, confused.

"It's right here." She ripped open a cardboard box and unhooked the machine's front panel to put the bottle in, crinkling her nose at the smell. She closed the panel and wiped her hands on her jeans.

"You're Beanie's cousin, huh?" he said, feeding papers into the machine. He squinted up at her. "You know, come to think of it, you remind me of Beanie. She's the soul of practicality. But Sara, why did you choose a psychiatrist who's related to you, more or less?"

"Look, maybe I *should* go to someone else," she said. He seemed to be a real flake, and now she thought maybe he wasn't worth her mother's money.

"No," he barked, gathering up the papers that the machine had spit out. Suddenly he became another

61

person entirely. "Our session has begun. Repairing this machine was part of it, for reasons I shall divulge later."

He trotted back to his office and Sara jogged behind, protesting. "Oh, you make everyone fix a Xerox machine, huh? Is this a new school of therapy? Jesus. You should be paying me." He ignored her, which made her feel rather relieved. She had never talked back to a shrink, and she wasn't sure what the consequences could be. But even as she ranted at him, she reminded herself that as long as she got Prozac, it would be worth dealing with this guy. Besides, the session was shaping up to be more interesting than the standard hour of chrome chairs and significant pauses you get with MDs.

He settled behind his desk and gestured for Sara to sit opposite him.

"Look," he said, "if you really are like Beanie, you hardly need my help. So tell me why you're here."

"My mom wants me to get Prozac." Sara told him about her mother, the miraculous cure. "Do you think I should go on it? Would it help me?"

He held up one pudgy hand. "Hold on. First of all, this euphoria your mother is experiencing is probably temporary—it happens with some people when they go on the drug. Give her another month or two, and then we'll decide whether it helps her."

Sara felt a little gleeful at this, at the idea of her mother calling and cursing the drug. "You mean it will stop working?"

"It's good for some compulsives. But it helps people cope—no more than that."

"Well, should I take it then?" Sara leaned forward. She was almost afraid to hear the answer. Somehow, she felt this was the moment of judgment, when he decided whether she was beyond hope or not.

"What's wrong with you?" He crossed his fat legs and his glasses slid down his tiny, ill-formed nose.

"I'm not happy."

"And what on earth does that mean?" He leaned over the desk, screwing up his shrewd eyes.

"I don't know. I'm just not."

"Well, do you make it to your job on time? Are you in danger of harming yourself or others? Are you capable of having sexual relations? Do you eat and sleep normally? In other words, do you behave like a healthy person?"

"Well, yes, but . . ." She didn't know exactly where this was leading.

"Then it sounds as if you can do quite well without Prozac, and even better without me," he said with a little slap on the table and a dismissive tilt of his head, as if he expected her to jump up and leave the office that moment.

"Wait. I don't believe this." Sara heard her voice get loud. "That's not professional. You can't just spend ten minutes with me and say I'm fine."

"You can cope. Most of my patients cannot. My colleagues seem to think it's their job to ensure their patients' happiness. But, Miss Baker," Sara was not sure when he'd switched to her last name, "happiness is

63

something that cannot be measured, cannot be defined. It's one of the great mysteries. Certainly it's beyond the scope of psychiatry. My job is to get people up and running, so to speak, as when you fixed that Xerox machine. I see a person flashing E5 and I give him or her toner. But I don't see you flashing anything, Miss Baker."

"But," Sara said, still puzzling over this analogy, "I've been to forty shrinks and not one of them ever said I was normal." It was really thirty, of course, but forty sounded better.

"Forty shrinks, forty winks," he said, almost to himself, then louder: "Look, if we could measure happiness, if it were something real, it's quite possible that you might be the happier of the two of us. But happiness aside, I think you can survive admirably, unlike myself. Certainly you can fix a Xerox machine, which is beyond me, and you probably wouldn't lose your patients' records as I do. So the idea of your paying me a generous sum for consultation is rather ridiculous, don't you think?"

WHEN SHE CAME out of the building, Andy was already waiting. She got in his car and slammed the door behind her.

"Well," he said, driving down the hill, "did you get it?"

"Yeah." She waved the piece of paper with the prescription on it so he was almost afraid it would fly out the window. "But it probably won't work and it costs a dollar a pill. I'm not even sure if I'm covered for it. And if I take it, I have to see that quack every month."

Andy leaned forward to look both ways, and then swung the car out onto the highway. "So he did think you needed it, huh?"

"No," she sniffed in a way that told him she was trying to recover her dignity. "He says I'm fine. I guess compared to him, I am. He's a total nut."

"So, but, he gave you the prescription anyway?"

"Yeah. He says I should decide for myself, but his professional opinion is that I should take all the money it would cost and put it in an IRA. As if I had the money in the first place."

"He said that?" Andy thought she was kidding, but when he glanced over at her, she was gazing earnestly at the piece of paper she had flattened out on her lap.

65

"What does it say, exactly," he nodded at her lap.

"I don't know. Latin," she said without lifting her head, as if she couldn't stop staring at it. "I wish I could read it."

They paused at a red light beside the river, and she watched how the water glared in the sun and then turned translucent brown as it passed under the shadow of the trees. Suddenly, her disappointment was tremendous, unbearable. "They never make it anything you can read," she said again, feeling her eyes get teary. "So you can't even understand what's going on inside you when you take it. The worst part is, they don't even know what it does to you themselves."

"Well, are you going to get it?" Andy said, quite reasonably, because he was used to the way she got worked up about things like this. It was nothing against him. "Should we go by a drug store?"

The light changed and he drove on.

After a few minutes, she said, almost whispered, "I don't know." When she looked over at him, he was leaning down to fiddle with the radio knob. As was his habit when they couldn't decide where to go next, he'd turned off a side street to drive in circles through the suburbs.

A strange idea occurred to Sara: Perhaps what she'd always thought of as dullness in Andy was happiness—not the kind of ecstatic happiness she and her mother had sought, the kind you could point to, that made you dye your hair blond and get a set of business cards printed. Andy's happiness wasn't in anything he did as much as the way he did it. Even now, he seemed content to drive aimlessly until she told him where to go. It was then she decided to ask his advice. It would be the first time she had ever done so.

"Andy, should I? Is it worth it?" she said, her voice sounding oddly tender. It seemed to her that she was asking him some larger question than whether she should take the pill.

He switched off the radio, as if to concentrate. "Hmm. Well, let's see," he said, and he turned onto a wide, shady street that neither of them knew.

The Underwear Man

MISS PAGE PINNED a note to my sweater. It looked like the white flower my father wore on his jacket on Sundays, but it smelled like penicillin.

The next week, I had to have X-rays. A nurse took me into a dark room and told me to sit on a metal table. She gave me a milkshake to drink. But it wasn't a milkshake; it wasn't even cold. Then the nurse told me to lie down.

She had curly hair that stayed stiff even when she moved her head, and she smelled like Band-Aids. She reached up and pulled down a machine so it hung over my stomach.

"You're going to have to lie real still so we can see your picture," she said. "Pretend you're a statue. Are you a statue?"

"Yes," I tried to say, but my mouth was dry and it came out in a whisper.

She moved the machine—black, with wires like whiskers—along my body, until it hung over my leg. She said, "Don't move your head, but look up. See that TV? That's you."

There was a TV hanging from the ceiling, but all that was on its screen was a white line inside a gray cloud.

"That's your leg," she said.

I closed my eyes tight—not wanting to, but thinking how my skeleton lived inside me. The skeleton was waiting until I died; then my skin would peel off and it would be born.

68

WHEN WE GOT in the car, I said, "Mommy, I don't want to go back there."

"I'm sorry, but you're going to have to," my mother said.

She twisted around to look behind her. She had her sunglasses on and instead of her eyes I saw myself with a huge forehead and tiny body.

"But Mommy, I don't want to." My voice sounded whiney, like it did when I was going to start screaming.

"Why not, sweetie?" she said.

The car was hot and smelled of the Coke that Jamie had spilled once.

"I had to look at my skeleton," I said.

We stopped at a light, and my mother touched me on the head.

"It's only a few more times," she said. "I'm sorry, but

we have to make sure everything's okay. Understand?"

The car turned and I was pressed against my seat. "I guess," I said.

I looked at my mother and she was moving her mouth like she did when she drove. The green arrow near the steering wheel was flashing, making the "tick tock, tick tock" sound. I hated that arrow, because when it blinked and made its sound, I had to breathe in time to it.

I wanted to tell her I had been to the room, though my skeleton wasn't on TV, it was real. It stood in front of me, its jaws clapping together to say words like "perambulator" and "jujitsu." Sometimes the room was sideways and my skeleton rolled toward me on wheels. Then I'd hear the tick-tock clicking of the green arrow. If I stopped breathing in time to the sound, even for one second, the skeleton would roll into me. It would hug me with its claws. It would press its skull against my face, pecking and pecking at my skin.

IN THE BACK of comic books, with the onion gum, remote-control ghosts, fake blood and dog whistles, I saw a pair of X-ray glasses. In the picture, a boy was wearing the round glasses, his eyes covered with spirals. His hair was standing on end as he looked at a woman and saw her skeleton.

Even though I didn't have the glasses, when I sat on my mother's lap, I could see the bones inside her legs.

WHEN I LAY in bed, I tried to keep my long hair tucked under my neck. I was afraid strands of it would fall over the edge of the bed, and a hand could reach up from underneath and grab it. Then I would wake up, feeling the tugging on my head, but it would be too late. I would be sliding over the edge of the bed. I would be pulled underneath, like water down a drain.

The worst was when the underwear man came. He creaked up the stairs, and then paced up and down in the hall outside my door. I lay with my arms straight and my eyes closed like a good girl, but that never made him go away. The door would open, and he'd come in; sometimes he walked all around the room, looking at my toys or in my closet. He wore a black cape, so all I could see of him were his eyes and his long nose. It always ended with him standing over me. After he stared for a while, he would bend exactly at the middle, till his nose was right over where my legs came together. He had X-ray eyes and could see through my covers. He was checking to see if I was wearing my underwear.

I made sure I always was, though my mother didn't want me to. She said that when you put on your nightie, you didn't need underpants, but I screamed if she tried to take them off.

Though I wore a clean pair of underwear to bed every night, I was scared every time he bent over me. If the underwear man had X-ray eyes, then he could see through my underwear, too. He might see through it by mistake and think I wasn't wearing any, or maybe a girl wearing underwear looked to him like a girl not wearing underwear.

ONE DAY WE went to the doctor's but I didn't have to lie in the dark with the machine over me. Instead, I sat on the table with the paper on it that rattled when I moved. My mother was in a chair, and the doctor, who had glasses that made his eyes look like guppies, was leaning against a counter. He said I'd have to be on crutches for a year.

"Mommy, I can walk fine," I said.

But it didn't matter.

That very day, we went to the crutch place. They had them there in all sizes, and I got the smallest—of light-colored wood, with pads on the arm rests that looked like rotten hot dogs. I wanted to take these off and play with them, because I thought they might float in the bathtub.

71

My mother knelt down to talk to me. She said, "No point in your going back to school today. Do you want to go for a milkshake?" I said I wanted to go to the park. Usually she would have said we had errands; usually, she was busy keeping Jamie from slamming his finger in the car door or eating gum off the sidewalk, but Jamie was at nursery school.

We went out onto the sidewalk. She walked slowly so I could keep up, watching to make sure I used the crutches right. I loved to have her watching me.

When we got to the park no one else was there.

"I want to swing," I said, and she helped me onto the swing. I had dropped the crutches, and they lay crossed on the wood chips. She pushed, and after her hands left me I could still feel the place where they had touched my back.

I WAS ALONE in the house and the phone rang. The man said, "Is your mother home, this is her doctor."

"No," I said.

"Well, then I'd like to ask you some questions. I just need to get some things straight. Is that all right?" He talked the way doctors do, as if he didn't really care.

"Yeah."

"What's your name?"

"Vicky."

"Okay, Vicky, how old are you?"

"Seven," I said.

"Now, Vicky, will you take some deep breaths for me?"

I breathed slowly, in and out.

"Very good, Vicky, you sound fine. Now, can you tell me what you're wearing?" he said.

"Jeans and a T-shirt."

"All right, now will you do something for me?" he said.

"Yeah."

"I want you to unbutton and unzip your jeans, okay?"

I tried to breathe in but my throat was stopped up. "Okay," I said.

"Now, Vicky, can you pull down your underwear for me?"

"Okay," I said when I had done it. My jeans and underwear were halfway down my legs. Then I re-membered the next-door neighbors might see me

72

through the window. I wanted to go stand behind the table, but I couldn't walk with my crutches when my pants were around my knees like that. So I stood there, right in front of the window.

"All right, Vicky, stick your finger in the place between your legs, okay? Do you know what that place is called?"

"No," I said. More than anything I wanted him not to say the name of it, I wanted not to know.

"Vicky, it's called a vagina. Now rub your finger around in there. Can you do that for me?"

I tried to say, "okay," but no sound came out.

"What Vicky? What did you say?"

"Yes," I croaked.

"Good. Now keep rubbing your finger around while we talk. All right, can you tell me something else? Have you ever seen your mommy and daddy doing anything funny together in bed?"

"No," I said. But when he said that, it made a picture come into my head of them looking at each other and laughing with their mouths so wide their faces were almost splitting.

"Now tell me something," he said. "Does your mother wear bikini underwear?"

"I don't know," I said.

"Do you know what that is, bikini underwear?"

"No," I said, even thought I sort of knew.

"It's a top part for your breasts and a bottom part for your vagina."

"Oh," I said.

"Do you wear it?" he said.

"No," I said. I was feeling bad, because I wasn't rubbing my finger like he had told me. I was afraid he would ask about that again.

But instead he asked, "I want you to do one last thing? Can you do that, Vicky?"

"Yes," I whispered.

"Vicky, take your finger out of your vagina. Have you done that?"

"Yeah." More than anything, I wanted to pull up my jeans, to move away from the window.

"All right, put your finger up to your nose, okay? Vicky, what does your finger smell like?"

I lifted my hand and the crutch I'd been leaning on with that arm clattered to the floor. I sniffed, but all I could smell was the salty smell of skin. I couldn't think how to answer at first. Finally I said, "nothing."

"Nothing, Vicky? Nothing at all?"

"Yeah, nothing," I said.

"Well, then, that's it, Vicky. Now remember to tell your mom I called, okay?"

"Okay," I said. I hung up the phone and pulled up my jeans.

When my mom came home, I said, "The doctor called."

"Which doctor?" she said. She was holding two grocery bags.

"I don't know."

"Did he say his name?" she asked, as she walked to the kitchen to put down the bags. When she asked this question, I knew that I'd just been a very bad girl.

I looked in the grocery bag on the floor so she wouldn't see my face. "No," I said.

THAT NIGHT, I knocked on my parents' door, crying. My mother knelt down next to me. She smelled like a person who's been sleeping.

"I had a nightmare. I dreamed I was scared and I came to your room, but when I looked in, you were both skeletons."

"Well, I suppose you can come sleep with us for a while," she said.

Really, I'd made up the nightmare so she'd let me in bed with them. I climbed in beside my sleeping father with the pillow over his head, and my mother lay down next to me. Soon she was asleep too. I thought I would be safe there, with my parents like walls around me.

Still, I was afraid when I heard the stairs creak, and then him walking down the hall. I hoped I had fooled him, that he would go into the other room and stand over my empty bed.

But my parents' door opened and I saw him like a shadow against the light in the hall. He slid across the room toward the bed.

I grabbed my mother's arm, but it was too heavy to lift. As he reached the side of the bed, I knew that I would not be able to wake her or my father.

He curled over me like a wave, rushing me into a dark place where I couldn't breathe. For the first time, I heard him make a sound. He sniffed. He had followed me here by my smell, because my stink was

75

all wrapped around our house: already my skin was rotting away, stinking up everything.

He peeled my skin off me like wet clothing, until my bones lay bare on top of the sheets. My bones were as white as teeth that have been brushed by a good girl, who does it just the way the dentist shows her.

The Tunnel

THE BOY WAS running through the tunnel when the bus came. He wedged himself against the wall, waving his arm in the spotlight of its headlights, but the bus didn't slow down. In fact, it hit the arm, so that later he lost it. There was a picture of him, when he still had both arms, in the paper—it must have been a school picture because his hair was combed and he was wearing a tie. He was pretty old, maybe fourteen.

"Terrible," my father said. He handed the paper across the breakfast table to my mother. "You're not to go near there. Not even near, you understand?" my father said to me.

I promised not to, but when my parents weren't watching, I picked up the silver napkin ring in front of my place and put my finger through it, pretending my finger was the boy and the napkin ring the tunnel.

I hadn't thought much about the tunnel until just then; it was something to concern older kids, who ran through it as a shortcut to the People's. That was the only place to hang out, a strip of stores—gas station, Safeway, pizza place and People's—along the Potomac. I was allowed to walk there; you followed wide, rutted roads winding up a steep hill and then down again: about a half-hour's walk. The tunnel bored straight through the hill.

After breakfast, I went over to Anne's house. She was sitting on her front steps eating a bowl of cereal.

I said, "I'm not allowed to go near the tunnel, my father just said." We began talking of other things, while picking the red berries off a bush that grew against the steps. Pretty soon, though, Anne set her bowl down on a stair and we began walking.

WE STOOD IN the shade, listening to the buzzing of locusts, which sounded like ripping paper. Down the road maybe fifty yards, the hill rose, a big hump blocking out the blue sky. The tunnel was a black hole in the hill, ringed with cement. A ways above it, there was a place where the tall trees had been cut down, the land flattened. There I could see into a backyard, the blue metal of a swing set, a Big Wheel lying on its side, the railing around a deck. The tunnel seemed out of place—a hole in the middle of the suburbs. It reminded me of how, when you held a paper tube next to your hand and looked through the tube with one eye, you could see a dark hole going through your palm.

"If I'm not supposed to go near it, how near is near?" I asked Anne, who was a year older.

"We're still far," she said.

We walked slowly toward it. I felt it pulling at me with a force like suction. The street forked: one way was a gravelly road; the other way, the pavement turned hard and black before it disappeared into the tunnel. We got onto the grass to walk beside the tunnel road. It was lined on each side with a wall of concrete almost as high as my shoulders, blindingly white in the sun.

"I think I should go back," I said. "I'm already too close."

"No, you'll only be near if you go over the wall," she pointed at the concrete next to her, "or even if you touch it." We had stopped near where the road disappeared into the tunnel. She hoisted herself up onto the forbidden wall and sat facing me. "You can sit there," she pointed to a shady spot of grass.

A sign outside the tunnel said, "Absolutely No Automobile or Pedestrian Traffic Allowed." Anne said "pedestrians" meant motorcycles.

EVERY FEW DAYS, we came back. Once we heard the tunnel start to whisper, as if it were talking to us, and then rumble, and finally the sound became so loud that Anne jumped off the wall. A bus burst out. It lumbered past us, bounced along the road, turned, and stopped to spit out a few people. It looked utterly ordinary, not like a thing that could rip off a boy's arm.

It was a few minutes after that when another boy came. We were sitting—Anne on the wall, me on the grass—and he walked out of the woods toward us. He was older than both of us, maybe twelve, a few inches taller than Anne, and wore cut-offs, basketball sneakers and an old T-shirt. He had a haircut just like Peter Tork in the Monkees.

He said, "Y'all going to run through the tunnel?"

"Maybe," Anne said.

"I'm going to," he said. "I live right up there," he pointed up to the hill, "and we run through it all the time."

"Really?" Anne said. I wished I were sitting up on the wall with her, looking just as cool, and suddenly I became aware of the way I was dressed—in shorts my mother had picked out, lime green with pink ladybugs all over them. Anne was wearing hand-me-down cut-off shorts like the boy's.

"Okay, listen up," he said. "Probably we're okay since a bus just came, but you still have to run the whole way, just in case." He was talking more to Anne, so I got up and stood closer to her. "But if one does come, you'll know 'cause you can hear it a million miles away. Then what you do is—well, there are these holes in the wall, they're like doorways—so if you hear anything, just run like crazy for the nearest one and get in there."

Anne said, "Why do you have to do that? It looks like there's tons of room for the bus to go around you."

He leaned forward, scratching at the ground with a stick as if making a diagram. "Yeah, but the buses can't really see you. Plus, if there's two buses going opposite ways, there's just room for them to get by each other.

If you couldn't get to a hole in time, one of them'd have to run you down."

I tried to catch Anne's eye, but she was looking straight at that boy.

"Let's go," he said. He vaulted onto the wall, and jumped down onto the road.

"Come on," Anne said to me.

I thought that if I touched the concrete wall, my father, miles away in his office, would look up from his work, knowing I had broken my promise. Even so, I took a step forward and put my hands against the concrete, which felt rough as a scab.

I hoisted myself up onto the wall and sat there for a minute. On one side of me was grass, still flat in the spot where I had been sitting; on the other side was the road, black and blank, disappearing into the tunnel. Anne jumped down onto the road, and after a second I did too.

She, the boy and I stood there for a minute, dazed by the heat rising from the road. My legs felt all rubbery because I knew I'd have to lie to my father that night. It was no good lying to him: he could read my mind. I'd say the lie, maybe I'd even have almost convinced myself it was true. But then he'd say, "You're lying, aren't you?" and I'd realize I was. He'd say, "What if you told us you were going into the backyard to play when you were really going down to the river, and then you fell in? We wouldn't know where you were; we wouldn't be able to help you. See, a lie separates you from us." I didn't understand that—about the lie separating me. When he said it, I pictured myself having to move into my own house where I'd live all alone.

We walked to the mouth of the tunnel. Because of the light from outside, you could see the first twenty feet or so, but after that the walls faded into darkness. From the ceiling some kind of moss hung, like stalagmites. Far away was a needle of white light.

The boy said, "On your mark, get set, go," and he and Anne took off. I, always slow to grasp things like that, hesitated, and then ran, trailing behind them. Our loud feet echoed with a metallic sound, and ahead of me the other two had turned into ghosts, gray and faded, bobbing up and down. The tunnel smelled of damp cement and motor oil.

We ran in single file, close to the wall. The boy yelled, "See?" and his voice echoed, as if there were boys hidden everywhere in the darkness. He raised his arm—a pale shadow—to point at the wall. Nothing could have gotten me to lift either of my arms in this tunnel. As I ran past I saw what he was pointing at, an arched, dark hole in the wall.

After we had run past several more of these doorways, it became so dark I could barely see the wall anymore. It was like a dream: though I ran as fast as I could, I seemed to be wading along through the dark, as if, instead of air, I was trying to run through melted black rubber. It was so dark I couldn't even see my legs when I looked down. I was aware mainly of sounds— the crashing of my feet like something falling down stairs; my own breathing like my father sawing a plank in half.

The end of the tunnel was vividly bright against the darkness. There, glowing ahead of me, was a circle of the outside world—a lurid patch of green, a car flashing by. The circle lit up the walls so they looked like they began out of blackness. Anne and the boy were shadows against the light, and I was close behind them. When I looked down, I could again see my feet flash under me. It seemed to me that now—when I was almost safe—was when I'd hear the drone of the bus and see it block out the light as it roared toward me. I pictured the newspaper article about how I had died, and the newspaper on the doorstep of our house, and my father leaning to pick it up.

Then I was in the twilight near the mouth of the tunnel, and Anne and the boy ran into the sunlight.

83

A moment later, I slowed to a trot, the sound of my feet on the pavement changed, and then the sun hit my eyes.

The three of us walked onto the sidewalk, where there was a deserted bus shelter, all breathing hard and bent over. Anne dropped onto the bench and I beside her. I felt almost as if I would throw up, as if I were filled with black rubber. Anne's pupils were still dilated—two black tunnels into her head—and I knew mine must be the same.

The boy was still standing; already he had his wind back. His straight, too-long hair had fallen over his eyes, and he jerked his head so that the hair swung back, away from his face. "Well, I got to go buy some cigarettes. They got a machine over in front of the gas station," he said, as if he thought we might want cigarettes too.

He loped off, and Anne said, "That's a dumb thing to do. He shouldn't smoke." Her mother smoked.

"Yeah," I said, despite what I was thinking. I pictured the boy walking behind the gas station and into the woods, where I wasn't allowed without my parents. He'd run down the trail, his sneakers skidding, and then walk over the canal lock. On the still, brown water his reflection would appear as a twitching shadow, with pieces of trees rippling through it. He would walk along the towpath next to the canal, take out the cigarettes and put one in his mouth, then stand there, with the flat, mud-smelling canal on one side of him, looking to the other side, at the Potomac glittering below him. He'd watch the crazy water arching off the rocks to make lace in the air and spin downstream bubbled like spit, and then he'd light the cigarette, inhale, and blow out through his mouth, turning the air in front of him blue.

Later he'd run back through the tunnel, but Anne and I would take the long way, through the suburbs.

WHEN I OPENED the front door and heard my mother yell my name from the kitchen, I felt angry for some reason. Usually when I came back from People's, I liked to show her what I'd bought with my allowance. She'd hold the tiny plastic toys in her hand, touching each one softly.

I hesitated, then said, "Yeah?"

"Come on in here."

I went to the kitchen. She was patting meat down into a plate of flour. "Oh my, you're all sweaty. Where have you been?"

"People's."

"Peep holes, huh?" she said, pronouncing it the way she thought I pronounced it, which she thought was cute. "Well, Sweaty, why don't you go up and take a bath before dinner?"

"No," I said.

"You're cranky, aren't you?" she said. "You must need blood sugar; have some Hawaiian Punch."

I narrowed my eyes and said it in a whisper. "I don't want any."

I HID IN MY room when I heard my father slam the front door, and didn't come down until they called me. They were at the table when I walked in. I thought my father would be able to tell I had been through the tunnel just by looking at me. I crossed the room trying to remember how fast I had walked, where I had focused my eyes before I had run through the tunnel. I sat at my place.

"I hear you went to People's," my father said, his glasses shining so his eyes were white holes.

"Yeah," I said. My voice sounded too high.

"Did you have fun?"

"It was okay."

Suddenly I realized he couldn't tell. For the first time, there was a place in me my father couldn't see. What it felt like was another girl inside me, one that didn't come from my parents. When I looked to the side of my place mat, I saw her, a dull shadow reflected in the polished wood of the table.

"What did you buy?" he said, handing me my plate.

"Anne's brother drove us there, and he bought me an ice cream cone, but I dropped it on the ground and a dog ate it." I lied on and on and it was like singing, like the hymns we sang in church that went straight up to God.

Camp

THE OTHER GIRLS came from places like Georgia and Florida, and they wore pink nail polish on their toes. The shelves above their bunks bristled with curling irons, eyebrow tweezers, perfume, Q-tips, Lady Bics.

I'd been looking forward to camp as a place where nobody washed. I thought we'd be cooking out over fires and sleeping in the dirt, and I'd be able let my long hair get all tangled like a girl who's been raised by wolves.

As it turned out, the other girls read *Seventeen* and gave each other makeovers until our rough-hewn cabin smelled of baby powder and strawberry lip gloss.

They treated me kindly in their way—I was a kind of retard, since I didn't shave my legs or own makeup. My bunkmate, Marge, said, "I'm going to give you this comb. Always keep it in your back pocket, and whenever you're not doing anything, use it."

After lights out, they talked about boys. Then only our flashlights lit the cabin, spotlighting a face, the fold of a blanket, the rafters. Ginny—who was a head taller than any of us—had let a boy feel her up, had played Seven Minutes in Heaven at a party once. And Marge had an actual boyfriend. They were our panel of experts.

One time Marge and Ginny argued about whether French kissing was first or second base.

"If it's second base, then there's more than four bases," Ginny said. So they agreed French kissing was first-and-a-half base. Suddenly I understood: sex was as difficult and abstruse as calculus. You had to work up to it slowly, in stages—holding hands was like addition; necking was multiplication; petting was trigonometry.

My only experience at all with boys was the few times I'd slow-danced. The boy and I would hold each other gingerly, not daring to lean together. And I hadn't even ever slow-danced to the important song yet, "Stairway to Heaven."

I wanted to be like Marge and Ginny. I wanted to be even more experienced than they were. And if I were, I wouldn't tell everyone about it after lights out. I would brood. I would be a fallen woman.

I was thinking a lot about fallen women because of a book, called *Sweet Stranger*—stained, dog-eared, with the back cover missing—that was being passed around the cabin.

Melanie, the heroine, falls off her horse, and this guy with a whip finds her and carries her on his shoulders to his plantation. He nurses her back to health—mainly by wiping her face with a cloth a lot. One day, he can't resist taking her in his viselike arms and kissing her violently. Soon after, she becomes a fallen woman.

I studied *Sweet Stranger* as if it were a textbook. Back at home, I was the best in my class at math and this had warped my mind. I thought I could master any area of life just by careful application of logic.

At first, in studying to become a fallen woman, I wouldn't even need an actual boy. After the others had gone to sleep—wrapped up in white sheets like cocoons—I lay awake and ran through my own version of *Sweet Stranger*. The man with the whip became a boy with thick glasses and clammy skin who read science fiction. A tree had fallen on him while he was sitting under it reading *The Martian Chronicles*—his legs were pinned underneath. I had to roll the tree off his legs and help him limp to safety. Later, I would visit him and sometimes when his mother left the room, I'd lie in bed with him, next to the leg in the cast, and we'd kiss. He'd put his hand up my shirt. Marge said you were supposed to say no, but I'd let him. That's the kind of girl I was.

IT WAS SATURDAY afternoon, and instead of being down at the lake for our swimming lesson, we were inside with all the curtains down. The other girls were giving each other makeovers, examining their

89

faces for pimples, using a cigar-shaped stone to file off the dead skin on their feet. That night was the first square dance with actual boys.

I lay on my bed reading, and for a while no one noticed me, but then Ginny said, "What about Helen? She can't go with her hair like that."

I looked up. "It's okay," I said. But it was too late.

"We should cut it," Marge said, looking at me with her hands on her hips, her eyes squinted. "Don't you want your hair cut? Like, shoulder length, with bangs feathered back."

"Yeah, and a makeover," someone said.

"You want us to do it?" Ginny said.

"I guess."

90

I didn't understand how this would help; surely, if a boy didn't like me, it would be for things the other girls would never be able to change—my stubby fingers, pale skin, flat chest, the large mole on my cheek. In fact, my only asset, I had thought, was the long, white-blonde hair they were going to cut off.

Still, I liked to have them stand around discussing my hair, my fingernails, my skin tone.

I sat in a chair in the middle of the cabin, and Marge cut. Debby put on makeup. She knelt over and brushed blush on my cheek. It felt good and I wanted to close my eyes, but I didn't or she might think I was queer.

They went through my trunk, but I didn't have any of the right clothes, so they dressed me in someone's designer jeans and low-cut T-shirt.

Finally they let me look in the mirror. I had sleek,

shoulder-length hair, a shirt that clung to my flat chest, and red lips. I was vaguely proud that all along I could have looked like them if I had wanted to.

THE LODGE WAS a long, dark building, which, despite its screen windows, still smelled of the meat loaf we'd had for dinner. Everywhere there were girls in makeup and designer jeans with combs in their back pockets and I was one of them.

The boys stood on the other side of the room. I hadn't seen a boy in two weeks. I had forgotten how loud they were. They slapped each other on the back and yelled. They tried to jump on the window ledges; they thumped, bumped, laughed, shouted. You could smell their sweat from across the room.

Marge took my arm. "Look at that guy. He's cute. He looks like my boyfriend." She pointed over at the boys, but I couldn't see which one she meant. They all looked alike to me in their own equivalent of our uniform: Levis, T-shirts, running shoes. Right then I gave up. There was no science fiction boy here.

We square danced to recorded fiddle music, one of the counselors doing the calling. It wasn't like a school dance, where no one danced. The boys had to ask us or they'd get bawled out by their camp director.

It wasn't until I'd gotten used to all the boys that I was finally able to ignore them—like a dense fog—and spot him. He was leaning against the wall, his face pressed to the screen window, as if fascinated by the view of pine tree branches. Though I wanted to, I never would have dared to do that—stand by myself in the middle of a dance.

I suppose I should have admired him for doing what I was afraid to, but instead I felt a sort of superiority. The idea that he was even more of a reject than I was, I think, was what gave me the courage to go over to him.

Even so, my embarrassment was so intense as I walked from the girls' side to the boys' side that I felt pinpricks all along my back, the same as when I was going to throw up. I was intensely aware of everything—how the white reflections on the floor followed me across the linoleum, the rise and fall of voices, the smell of the boys. I approached him in a sickening slow motion, like the part in scary movies where the killer is stalking.

"Hi," I said, and he turned.

He had greasy hair that fell past his ears and aviator glasses, and he wore a button-down shirt instead of a T-shirt.

"Hi." He had a slight stutter.

That made me brave. Suddenly, in the makeup and the new haircut, I felt disguised. For all he knew, back home I might be popular. Maybe I had come over to him just because I felt sorry for him.

"You want to dance?" I said it cool, as if some counselor had made me.

He said okay, and so we shoved our way through the boys out onto the empty floor, where he stood beside me, hands in his pockets, looking down.

"What's your name?" I said.

"Jim." He glanced up for a second, squinting at me.

I could feel myself assuming a personality not at all my own: I had convinced myself that I was like one of those girls at the roller rink at home. Sometimes when she went shopping, my mom left me and my friend Anne at the rink. We didn't skate much; mainly we drank Cokes and watched the girls our age, who wore tons of makeup and tight jeans. Their boyfriends were older, with faint mustaches and blow-dried hair like Scott Baio. When the DJ played "Disco Lady" or "Shake Your Booty," they'd sing along to prove they knew all the words. And when we went in the bath-room, they were sitting on the counter and smoking. Once I looked at one of those girls too long, and she said, "What the fuck's your problem?"

93

Now I adopted the world-weary attitude of a roller rink girl. I said, "Hey, there's Marge—she's my bunk-mate. Look at her flipping her hair around. She's so weird."

"Where?" he said.

"Over there, in the yellow shirt." I was afraid that he was one of those people who didn't like to say bad things behind other people's backs.

But, after a minute, he seemed to catch on. He pointed, "That's my bunkmate. They call him 'Beef.' He wants to join the army." Along with his stutter, Jim had a deep-South accent. This too gave me confidence.

I started laughing. "Beef! I can't believe that." I was laughing too hard, aware of how fake I was being.

He laughed, too, awkwardly, as if someone had once told him he looked stupid when he laughed.

"Okay, you all," the counselor yelled, "get on out there." There was a flurry of partner-choosing, and then the fiddle music started. We do-si-doed, two-stepped, whirled in circles, bowed to each other in squares. Jim, of course, was an awkward, shuffling dancer with sweaty hands.

When we promenaded around the room, I said, "I hate camp. It's like one long gym class."

"It's not so bad," he said. "I like to walk around in the woods. I go to shop and they let me read."

"What are you reading?"

"*The Hobbit.*" ·

"Wow, me too." Actually, it wasn't so surprising. It was the summer every twelve-year-old math whiz in America was reading *The Hobbit*. Somehow I'd convinced myself that I was a brainy roller rink girl—I was the kind teachers said would have great promise if they could only reach me.

Between dances, I kept him talking about the book. He spoke with his head down, aiming his remarks at my feet. He had a habit of crossing his arms on his stomach, as if trying to hold in his guts, that I found charming.

Finally there was an intermission and we stood next to one another, confused. I wanted to ask him to sit down, but I didn't know how to do that without making it obvious I liked him.

Marge ran up from behind me. "Helen," she giggled, "did you see that guy I was dancing with?"

94

"No, which one?" I said, panicking as Jim drifted away.

"That guy over there. You know what he said?" She leaned close to me.

"Wait a sec," I said, "I have to go to the bathroom really bad." I snaked my way through the crowd and found him leaning against the wall, looking out the window.

"Let's go sit on the benches," I said.

We sat on an empty bench behind a speaker, Jim a safe distance from me. Some boys ran by us, leaving their horsey smell.

"Did your parents send you to camp, or did you want to go?" I asked.

"It wasn't like that," he clutched his stomach. "My guidance counselor at school said I spend too much time alone. He said I should go to camp to learn how to deal with people better."

This admission made me embarrassed. I wished he would play it cool like the other kids. I could see what the guidance counselor wanted him to learn—how to lie, how to put on an act.

"Well, are you learning anything?" I said, sarcastically.

But he answered sincerely, "I think. Sometimes the other kids and stuff are really nice to me. Like, even Beef and me hang out sometimes. It's different than school—people are really nice."

Suddenly the thought of getting him to seduce me seemed exhausting. From the way my cabinmates talked about it, you had to fight the boy off like a dog

95

trying to hump your leg. I didn't know that he would confide in me. I had no idea my skill at math would be useless.

THE NEXT SQUARE dance was at Camp Toma-hawk, which was much cornier than ours. Their lodge was called "Hootenany Hall"; the girls' bathroom had a sign on it made out of wood and shellacked rope that said "Squaws"; and they had a real square dance fiddler, an old guy wearing a polyester cowboy shirt. I didn't see how Jim could face all this with sincerity—could really think he was there to learn; but when I looked across the room, he was sincerely wearing a nametag right over his heart. Most of the other boys had put theirs on their stomachs or legs.

We didn't get a chance to talk—the caller kept us whirling around until we were shining with sweat—but when the counselors herded us outside to stand in front of the flag and sing Taps with our hands on our hearts, we stood next to each other and Jim let his hand slip off his heart to dangle near my arm.

On the van ride home, Marge said, "Who was that guy?"

"Just this guy," I said. I thought she would make fun of him because he wore retarded clothes.

But to Marge, a boy was a boy. She said, "He really likes you. Were you holding hands?"

"Sort of," I said. Now everyone in the van was looking at me. "Except, we didn't actually touch."

After that, getting Jim to seduce me was no longer my own personal burden; in fact, I had little say in the matter.

WHEN THE BOYS filed in, Ginny held me by the shoulders. "Go on, hurry up," she said. They'd decided I had to get him outside. We were allowed to go out in front of the lodge as long as we didn't step off the flagstone patio into the woods. You always heard about kids who'd been caught necking outside—older kids—but as long as they had their feet on the flagstones, they didn't get in too much trouble.

I found Jim over by his window, where he was using a magnifying glass to look at his hand.

"Hi," I said.

He looked up slowly, putting the magnifying glass in his shirt pocket. "Hi, Helen. How're you doing?"

"Hey, let's go outside," I said, as if it had just occurred to me.

We went out and sat on the fence around the patio, under the bell they rang to call us to dinner. The sun had just gone down and the whole sky was a faint pink, the same color as his skin. I could see blue and green veins through his cheek. He sat nearer to me now, not even a foot away.

"I'm in a play," I said. "It's kind of stupid—you know, it's about something that happens in Toy Town. But it's kind of fun, I guess."

"That's great." He looked straight at me until I got uncomfortable and looked away. "I've been doing a lot of stuff in art class, a couple of paintings. And I made you something." He reached into his shirt pocket.

It was a piece of sea glass—or lake glass, I guess—a misty green, wrapped in a spiral of silver wire and attached to a leather thong. There was the same beauty in the necklace as in the green veins that showed through his skin just under his ear. "Wow," I said, and put it around my neck. "That's pretty cool. It looks like it comes from Middlearth."

His gift made things seem serious, and I searched for something serious to say. "I didn't know you liked art. Is that what you want to be?"

"No, I want to be an engineer," he said.

I was relieved. I didn't like the kids in school who hung out in the art room. They didn't have the proper discipline of mind. "What kind?" I said.

"Robotics. I've already built a robot. I mean, it's just an arm actually. It still doesn't even work." As he told me about it, he talked faster, lost his stutter. He was like the boy assistants on Mr. Wizard that I always got crushes on. The more he got absorbed in telling me about capacitors and shut-off switches and conductors, the more I wanted to touch his hand only a few inches away from me on the fence.

Just then, a counselor came by and said, "Come on y'all, we're starting." The girls who'd been playing hopscotch on the flagstones went inside.

"I don't want to go in there," I said.

"Me neither."

"How about I show you around our camp?" I jumped off the fence. He followed, but only to the edge of the flagstones—he knew the rule, too. I stood at the beginning of the pine needle path that led down to the lake, but he hovered behind me, at the edge of the patio, with his hands in the pockets of his jeans.

I had never touched him except when we were square-dancing, and as I reached my hand toward him, I felt like I was about to barf. It was as if I were watching myself from outside, the better to see how dumb I looked, a girl with stubby fingers and a huge mole on her cheek.

I touched his arm at the wrist and, amazingly, he took his hand out of his pocket and held my hand. We stood stiffly like that for a minute. "Come on," I said, pulling, and he followed me.

It was getting darker. The pine needles were slippery, and there were roots and rocks in the path. For a while, all we said was, "Watch out" and "Careful." The music from the lodge had grown faint, and the crickets loud. I knew from science class that their song was a mating call; because he must know this also, I blushed.

Our hands were getting sweaty, but neither of us changed our grip—to do so would be to go through the whole embarrassment again. We stopped in a clearing and I pointed to a dark gap in the trees. "Down there's my cabin. All of the cabins have stupid names and ours is Lakeview. We call it Le Puke."

His voice sounded hoarse and out-of-breath. "I've never done anything against the rules like this before, you know."

"You must have broken some rules," I said. "Everyone does." For me (the roller rink girl) sneaking out of a square-dance was small-time compared to, say, stealing a carton of cigs from the rink snack bar. I was getting annoyed. Any normal guy would act like

99

ditching the square dance was no big thing, would maybe even brag about all the other millions of dances he'd snuck out of. But Jim was some kind of idiot when it came to playing it cool.

"Come on," I said, and half-pulled him down the path until we reached the lake. It lapped near our feet with little smacks that sounded like kisses. Far away, a fringe of trees blackened the other shore. Now the breeze was stronger, blowing the hairs on my legs the wrong way, making my shirt ripple against my stomach.

Still holding hands, we sat down on a long, flat rock, dangling our legs over water black as oil.

I said, "This is where we have corny 'Church in the Pines.'"

"Helen," he said, "have you ever had a boyfriend or anything?"

I heard my heart pound in my ears. "Yeah, I sort of had a boyfriend this summer before I came here, but then we had a fight." Actually, I had spent the first weeks of summer lying on my stomach reading *Little Women*.

"Well, I've never had a girlfriend or anything," he said. "I don't know what to do, or what to say or anything." His voice cracked.

I blushed and my stomach hurt. "Don't worry so much," I said. I wished a tree would fall on his legs so I could roll it off and cradle him in my arms—in the urgency of the situation, there would be no time for awkwardness. But there aren't any trees near the shore of a lake.

I wanted him to shut up. I just wanted to become a fallen woman without us having to discuss it every step of the way. So, without saying anything, I leaned my head against his shoulder. When I had done this in my imagination, the shoulder was like a pillow, but in real life it was hard, and had a bone that stuck into my jaw.

He stiffened. He was barely able to speak through his stutter. "Wait. I'm getting a stomachache." He did not let go of my hand, but with his free arm he clutched his stomach.

I had a terrible stomachache too. I would have liked it if I could have let go of his hand and doubled up into a fetal position, and if he had done the same, each of us balled up at separate ends of the rock. We would groan companionably, whining to one another, "Ugggh. I think I'm going to throw up. Oh, I feel so embarrassed." It would have been nice, but that was no way to become a fallen woman.

So I said, "It's okay. You don't have to get upset." I craned my neck upwards toward his face. At first he jerked away, but then we started kissing with our lips closed. I thought kissing was supposed to be so great, but it was like pushing my lips against slugs. I pictured a piece of paper like a shopping list, but it was the fallen woman list, and I was checking off the first thing on it, which was "kissing."

He drew away from me and started to say something, but I pushed his head down with my hand. I opened my mouth and our tongues touched. It was

101

horrible. Once, when I was a little kid, Anne and I had touched tongues so she could catch my cold. It was gross then and it was gross now—like eating slimy mushrooms. But I was able to check off "French kissing" on the list in my head.

He pulled away, catching his breath. "Are you crazy?" he said.

"That's what you're supposed to do. I swear. You're just not used to it yet."

"No way. You mean you really like that?" He slipped his hand away from mine and held his stomach with both arms.

"Sure," I said.

"I'm sorry," he said. "I just can't do that. I guess it's true what they said."

"What?"

He was looking away from me, at the dark shadow of the dock. I couldn't tell if he was crying. "I'm socially retarded."

The water heaved below us, smelling like mud, like swamps, like all the secret things.

I sighed, as if annoyed.

When he turned to me, he wasn't crying, but his jaw was tight, like someone waiting to be hit. He said, "I'm sorry. We can go back if you want."

I thought then of the lodge way above us on the hill, so brightly lit in this black forest of blasted logs; corpses of trees crawling with bugs; smells of tar, blood, mud, broken leaves; bats like crazy confetti. Up on the hill, the girls and boys wove between one another, each dancer like a number in an algebra

102

problem, partners changing to fill in the x and y of empty places.

"Yeah, I want to go back," I said, my voice cracking. He looked at me then. I think he got a glimpse of me then. I wanted to tell him. I was going to say, "I've kind of been making things up—lying—because I was afraid you wouldn't like me."

I could feel my heart beating in my whole body; even my feet pounded in my sneakers. I opened my mouth and took a breath. But when I spoke, I said, "Yeah, I'm going back." It was the bored, flat voice of the roller rink girl. She had taken my body; she had possessed me.

Slowly she stood up. Jim watched, his mouth twisted under the blank eyes of his glasses as she jumped from rock to rock, then stooped to pick something up. She cocked her arm and flung it expertly over the lake. After pausing to hear the far-away plop, to see the faint fireworks of it falling in the water, she said, "Later," and disappeared between the trees.

103

The Black Forest

THE PHILOSOPHY BUILDING was down a dirt road lined with pine trees that my friend Nira called "the Black Forest" after the region where Heidegger was born and later where the old Nazi hid as he waited for Germany to fall. When I walked through the Black Forest to class, the stunted trunks of the trees, the looming slate roof of the philosophy department and the gritty New England sky really did look blackened, the way they would in an old photograph. At these times, I'd hug myself tightly, clutching the folds of my coat, as if to hold all the pieces of myself together.

I was a freshman, just waking from a Protestant childhood of hot baths, horseback riding and pink-faced relatives who knew which fork to use. We went to church but never spoke of our God; he was so demonstrative and angry as to be an embarrassment to us. My life had been like Ohio: flat, but with a fast, sparkling river of doubt running through it. And when in a high school class the teacher read a sentence of Nietzsche's out loud—"Whatever a theologian feels to be true *must* be false: this is almost a criterion of truth"—I felt myself blushing, so exactly did it echo my forbidden thoughts.

Still, when I got to college, I registered as a math major. I'd won the math prize in high school and ever since had anticipated my life unfolding like an arithmetic progression: I'd get a PhD, become a professor, marry, have gifted children, die. I thought I'd be like my advisor, the token woman in the math department, who wore her hair short, punctuated her sentences with chopping motions and smelled of strong soap.

The first time I went to see her, she was sitting under a blackboard filled with formulas. We went over the catalogue and she circled the courses I should take—two maths, two sciences and German. I wasn't interested in these classes, but I signed up for all of them: I thought that if I followed her instructions, I'd finally be able to silence my doubts and lead the type of life expected of me.

Indeed, I went through the first week of school with the best of intentions, and I might have gone on with them had I not met Nira. She sat next to me in German, and I thought she was from a foreign country because she wore a tux jacket, bright red lipstick and her black hair in a cup around her head.

But after class, when I asked her where she was

from, she said, "West 83rd," and, seeing my confusion, added haughtily, "Manhattan." Then she leaned forward, as if no one else in the classroom must hear, and said, "I'm only taking this class because I'm in love with Kant. Reading a philosopher in the original is a deeply intimate experience, don't you think?"

"I've never tried," I said. "Which philosophers have you read in the original?"

"None, actually," she said, "but I'm planning to." Later I learned that Nira drooled over philosophers as if they were rock stars. She called the Young Hegelians the Hot Young Hegelians and had once propositioned the dying Sartre in a letter, to which she got no response.

Almost everyone had filed out of the classroom door and I was afraid she would leave, too, so I said, "Do you want to go somewhere and talk?"

She paused a minute and then said, "Okay, let's go have coffee at my house."

She lived in a duplex, students on both sides, and a heap of rusty bikes and decaying furniture on the porch. We sat in the kitchen, where the sun played over the cracked linoleum floor, and once in a while a car passed with a drone. Nira paced back and forth, smoking down a cigarette, while the coffee dripped into the pot.

When she asked, I listed my courses for her. "I'm a freshman," I added.

"No kidding," she said. "You've got freshman written all over you." I assumed she was alluding to my pink and credulous face, which I had inherited from a family that believed the world rewarded hard work and devotion to our stone-hearted God.

She poured the coffee and asked, "Well, how long is it going to take you to drop this math business, huh?"

"I like math," I said, taking the warm cup, but it sounded unconvincing. "It's like this very orderly world."

Nira sat down, wrapping her hands around her mug. "Well, you're fooling yourself. I've never lived in an orderly world and I never want to." This served as a launching point into her life story. Her mother was a dancer, her father an alcoholic. "Every time I got home from school it seemed there was some new drama: my mother had kicked my father out; or she'd gone to California; or both of them were there screaming at each other with the dog barking."

She wanted to know how I'd grown up, but I couldn't get it right. When I thought of home, I pictured the little boats moored in the lake, jostling each other in the wind; my mother reading to us at teatime; my father hunched over some papers in his study. Though we never wanted for anything, my parents, with their whispers late at night and their glances at each other over the morning financial page, seemed to believe we were on the brink of ruin. I said, "Our house faces the north and in the winter it's filled with this beautiful, gray light." I was remembering the way our table looked at Thanksgiving or Christmas, that stark light glancing off the crystal glasses, we with our heads bowed in dutiful prayer.

Nira pulled her knees up under her chin. "Go on,"

108

she said, "I'm finding this very interesting. I thought people like you only existed in *New Yorker* stories." And though she said little as I talked, I began to see my childhood as if it were someone else's, a curiosity.

When it began to grow dark in the kitchen, Nira snapped on the lamp. It held us both in its rosy circle of light. I was happy then as I watched her small hands fiddle with the cigarette pack and finally slide another one out; I was happy simply that she, for some inexplicable reason, had consented to be my friend.

"What are you going to do?" I asked her. "I mean, what do you want to do with your life?"

"My ambition," she said grandly, as she took a long drag from the cigarette, "is to be a bum. I won the freshman prize in philosophy; next year, junior year, they'll probably let me go to Germany on their special scholarship thing. But as soon as I get there, I'm going to drop out and live with the squatters and loot grocery stores. Why, what do you want to be?"

When I told her, she made a disgusted face. She said, "Look, Helen, I can see you have potential. Why just throw it away on being a math teacher?"

Then I knew she was right. When it came down to it, I had no interest in math or teaching. I couldn't even remember how I had come up with the idea. I pictured myself sitting in a cinderblock office grading papers while Nira threw a brick through a store window and ran down the nighttime streets of Berlin, her arms full of ill-gotten packages of coffee and cigarettes.

"Okay, math is boring," I said. "But what do I do? It's too late to change my classes this semester."

She said, "Well then, just stop going to class."

AS IT TURNED out, Nira was a grind. She told me she went to the library to seduce men, but when I visited her there, I found her already trying to read Wittgenstein in the original, her mouth chewing on the long words. I could never get her to do anything—she spent even weekend nights curled up on her sofa in the basement of the humanities library.

I did go to classes, but filled out my problem sets with a gleeful indifference that left me plenty of time for freshman antics. My hallmates and I traveled everywhere together in a large, boisterous group. We were all equally without friends and this had made us shameless. We sang in the streets, threw food, set off fire alarms.

In high school, I had hung out with the smart kids: boys who retold Monty Python jokes, girls who worked SAT words like "surreptitiously" into conversation. I was embarrassed by my smart friends, especially when the bad kids—wearing heavy-metal T-shirts and torn jeans, their pockets bulging with things I could only imagine—walked by us and burst out laughing.

I suspect that most of my hallmates had been smart kids, too, but free of our high school identities, we did our best to be bad. For instance, we kept a keg in one of the shower stalls. With the aid of this ready supply of beer, I lost my former shyness and became the wild girl I'd always wanted to be. I vomited on someone's bed; I slept with a boy from another dorm and then pretended not to know him. The semester passed in a giddy blur, like the trees and grass you glimpse when you're running down a hill drunk.

When Christmas break arrived, I was afraid to go home: I thought my parents would see immediately how I had changed. But, owing to my grades—an undeserved string of As and Bs—and my exhaustion, they assumed I'd been working harder than ever. My mother even said to me, "You look a little peaked. Do you get out and have some fun at school?"

Before I left for vacation, Nira had given me a worn copy of Nietzsche's *Genealogy of Morals*, and I spent the days before Christmas lying on my bed caught up in its blustery passages. I had grown accustomed to wildness at school, and Nietzsche's words stirred in me an inner wildness. I was blown about by that stormy prose like one of our little boats yanking at its rope in a strong wind. I can't say what tethered me to land, but it was a line that was sure to snap. At Christmas dinner, my head rang with Nietzsche's quote from the Turkish assassins he admired—"Nothing is true, everything is permitted"—and I offended an aunt by arguing along these lines.

Vacation for me was grueling, so long and wholesome. My younger sister and brother and I skated on the lake, long plumes of breath streaming behind us. But I was annoyed by their pink faces, pinker from the cold and the tightness of wool hats and scarves. With them, the conversation was all sleds and cranberry breads and frozen mittens. I imagined that Nira was standing on the ice beside us, smoking a cigarette and sneering.

So whenever Tim and Sally came to my room with their ice skates dangling from their hands, I told them to go on without me. Nietzsche wouldn't have gone skating. I knew this because I was reading his biography. His early life seemed, to my overwrought mind, an exact replica of my own. He was born to a bourgeois family, raised in a small and stifling town. Everyone, even Nietzsche himself, expected that he would become a minister. While he worked for his theology degree, Nietzsche plunged himself into the prostitutes and parties of fraternity life, but soon realized such decadence was only a distraction: he could no longer ignore his heady visions. So, despite his family's protests, he dropped theology and began to study for a philology degree.

His later life was murky. Though his work was well-received for a time, Nietzsche fell into darkness. The syphilis he must have contracted during a student fling had infected his brain. He was subject to fits of madness, vomiting, blinding headaches. He traveled ceaselessly— to the Swiss Alps and cities of Italy—all the while scribbling down aphorisms like claps of thunder among the storm of his sickness. After *Zarathustra* was met with indifference, he began to sign his letters "Dionysus." At the end, his mother cared for him. He played with dolls or just sat staring. But sometimes he'd open up that mouth and scream, as if he'd seen something terrible.

WHEN I GOT back to school I wanted more than anything to take the Nietzsche seminar, even though Nira warned me that I didn't have a chance of getting in. "Maybe," she said, "if you go over there right now and start groveling, the instructor will take pity on you."

I'd never been to the philosophy department. I expected something like the science department, an undistinguished building with fluorescent lights and modular furniture, so I was surprised when I saw it in the middle of the unkempt apple orchard, a Franken-stein castle with turrets and shingled roofs and narrow, leaded windows. The oversized door opened onto the front hall and a grand staircase with a fat balustrade. I wandered, lost in the chandeliered rooms and mir-rored hallways, until someone directed me to the basement.

At first I thought his office was the boiler room. It was under the stairs and too low to stand up in at one end. He was there, humming to himself and writing, behind a desk that just fit into the room.

"Mr. Shapiro?" I said, standing outside the door.

He looked up and I saw how young he was— certainly not much older than Nietzsche's twenty-four years when he was made a professor at Basel. His long hair was pulled into a ponytail and, behind gold-rimmed spectacles, his eyes were angry.

I told him I was a freshman, that I'd never taken any

philosophy, but that the *Genealogy* was the most important book I'd ever read.

"Your sincerity is admirable," he said dryly. "Why don't you sit down?"

I was forced to sit uncomfortably close to him and so became suddenly self-conscious about my pink face and the sweatshirt I wore, emblazoned with two crossed hockey sticks. He leaned close and I caught his smell of exotic tobacco. He said, "Do you believe that Nietzsche was an anti-Semite?"

I groped for the proper response. "I don't know much about it, except that he hated anti-Semites, even if at times he may have sounded like he hated Jews. It was just that his sister—"

114

"Good," he sat back, satisfied. "Well, there's always room for one more in the class," he said, and dismissed me.

I found Nira on her sofa in the humanities library. We went out to the lounge and I told her about my meeting with Mr. Shapiro. "That proves it," she said. "He's an apologist for Nietzsche. A Jewish apologist for Nietzsche."

"How do you know he's Jewish?"

She rolled her eyes. "His name." Nira was Jewish or half-Jewish, or something.

"Well, how come he can't admit that Nietzsche may have had a racist streak? How come he's obsessed with denying it?"

She stubbed out her cigarette. "Repressed masochism."

"SYPHILIS," MR. SHAPIRO said, and let the word hang in the seminar room. "Do you know about the ravages of syphilis?" He paced back and forth and then stopped to fix us with those angry eyes, as if we were somehow to blame. He went on to detail the symptoms—periods of excruciating sickness, and interludes of euphoric health during which the patient may have glimpses of a divine order. "Such was Nietzsche's condition. He can hardly be blamed if he got carried away, if he committed certain indiscretions."

I pictured Nietzsche as looking like Mr. Shapiro— who had the requisite handlebar mustache and wore an old-fashioned suit that drooped on his frail body. But Nietzsche's drama, I imagined, was my own. Like him, I'd had my brief period of decadence, but now I would turn inward, for I had come down with a syphilis of the soul. I understood that I was speeding toward a life of doubt and darkness, a Black Forest where each tree would stand for a blasphemy.

After class, I walked to dinner in a Wagnerian mist. I was attuned to the discordant music of a senseless universe as I crunched across the frozen snow of the football field. In the dining hall, I ate silently, my freshman friends giggling and gossiping around me.

My roommate, a bubbly girl who up until then I'd always liked, said, "Is something wrong?"

"No," I said, but walked back to the dorm alone, and packed everything I would need. While Nira had chosen the basement, I opted for the top floor of the

115

humanities library. I made myself a burrow behind one of the chairs, where I could see the window. From then on, I lived in a heap of paper coffee cups from the machine downstairs, extra sweaters, loose papers and Nietzsche books. My clothes had coffee stains like maps of imaginary countries all over them and there was a sour smell about me.

I discovered what Nira must have known all along—that there is a decadence in prolonged and overenthusiastic study. I drank as much coffee as I had alcohol the semester before, and kept the same hours, collapsing into my bed after the library closed at 2 A.M. I often thought with disdain about my freshman friends crawling the campus pub while I sat under the fluorescent lights of the library inching my way toward truth.

Mr. Shapiro had assigned *The Birth of Tragedy* and it was this book I read during those late nights, though I must admit I understood little of it.

The next week's seminar didn't help. Mr. Shapiro devoted most of class to one sentence that mentioned Semites. And the other students brought up questions as opaque to me as the reading had been. A boy smoking a clove cigarette asked if it was true that *The Birth of Tragedy* was philologically unsound. He was answered by a girl with thick glasses and no chin who argued against Nietzsche's use of the Greek word *agon*.

The next week, I went back to *The Birth of Tragedy* determined to understand it on my own. I read all the footnotes and looked up the strange words, but somehow I had only the vaguest sense of it, like a tune that

116

I couldn't quite remember. Still, just reading the strange words, even holding the book, sent my heart thumping.

I told Nira, "I understand what you meant about being in love with philosophers. I'm in love with Nietzsche, but it's torture. I feel like I'm going to burst, because he'll never be real. He'll always be words."

She said, "My God, Helen, don't take this so seriously or you're going to flip out."

But I did take it seriously. Up in my encampment on the top floor of the library, I'd stare out the window at the knuckled branches and, beyond, a slice of the Connecticut River, which in winter was the color of a slug. I'd read a few sentences of Nietzsche, but soon I was back to my question. Even at the time, I knew my question was philosophically weak. I had not defined my terms, built my question on the solid rock of a priori. Instead, I'd fixed on a string of words, like an incantation: "What is this thing?" By "this thing," I meant the whole tangled string of myself, tethered to another self as remote and unpredictable as a boat caught in a storm.

117

Though I still couldn't figure out the nuances of the Greek words, I thought I was beginning to fathom *The Birth of Tragedy*: It was about me. I had been brought up in Apollonian innocence, learning to dance in perfect diagrams, to win As in math, to accept my sunny future like a tautology. But inside me ran the red river of Dionysus, a madness of love I could fall into like someone's arms.

I often examined myself in the mirror of the library bathroom. I noticed with pleasure that my skin had lost its pinkness and turned dead white. My hair, once falling in neat waves down my back, was now a rumpled bundle piled up on my head. Sometimes my own reflection seemed terribly remote; I imaged that my body had its own life and that I was only a floating consciousness, a mind with no mooring.

Mr. Shapiro had assigned a short paper on *The Birth of Tragedy*, and I wanted to write something as brilliant and passionate as Nietzsche's own essays. So I began to work on a diatribe against the Apollonian, the way of math and logic and light.

When I told Nira about my idea she said, "Philosophy isn't confessional poetry. You have to be cool. You have to have an attitude. Write about how Nietzsche borrows from Schopenhauer's aesthetics, that's my advice."

I ignored her advice. When I stared out the window at the black branches quivering in the wind, I knew I was on the verge of some enormous revelation. I felt the pressure of it building inside me, the same way one feels the pressure of tears before they come, and readied myself for the flash of inspiration by jotting down ideas in English and German.

I was so caught up that I failed to go to my other classes. I slept in my clothes. I woke early and breakfasted in my room on a cup of instant, the granules of coffee floating on top because I had no spoon to stir them with.

And one day when Nira found me hunched on the

library floor, source materials scattered around me, she put her hands on her hips and pronounced proudly, "You're having a nervous breakdown."

I gazed up at her dully. "How can you tell?"

"You look like a wild animal or something." She sat down on the floor beside me. "Some kind of animal that makes its nest out of papers."

"I keep feeling like I'm going to cry," I said. My voice sounded creaky because I hadn't talked to anyone that day.

"Come on. It's time you got out of here. Let's go down to the Blue Bonnet."

As we walked down the hill to town, I looked around me at the thin, shivering shrubbery along the sidewalk, the parked cars coated with frost, the leaves eddying on the streets with little scratching sounds. These things amazed me with their ordinariness.

Despite the cold, we climbed the steps onto the suspension bridge, cars whizzing by us as we leaned over the railing. Below, the coal-colored Connecticut flowed between margins of ice.

If I fell in, I would be swept past the old factory buildings along the shore, my coat soaked with water. Slowly, I would be pulled down into the tarry depths of the river. I imagined it all vividly, as if I had already drowned. I began to cry, stabbing at my face with gloved fingers to wipe the tears.

I was embarrassed but, for my sake I think, Nira pretended not to see how I was wiping my face or hear me sniffing. She was leaning with her back on the railing, watching the cars. "It's too cold," she said.

119

"Let's go." Her words came out in ghosts of mist. I followed her over the train tracks and through a parking lot to the Blue Bonnet, a grimy diner with a plastic chicken in a blue hat that stood like a sentry beside the door.

We sat at a booth and a waitress poured our coffee. She was about our age, with hair permed into stiff curls, and she was still laughing at something the other waitress had said. It occurred to me like a revelation that here was this whole town and waitresses and old men sitting by the window and the cook somewhere making eggs and all of it went on without anyone thinking of Nietzsche.

When the waitress left, I said, "Most people just talk and eat and stuff without having to agonize every minute about whether they're doing the right thing with their lives—it's like they're on automatic pilot. But my automatic pilot has switched off. That's what's wrong with me."

Nira slowly slid a cigarette out of her pack and told me about *her* nervous breakdown. "I was afraid to move, so I just sat very still," she said, and explained that back then she'd imagined time as a mansion of halls and doors, a maze she no longer wanted to navigate.

"I just stopped making decisions," she said, dribbling cream into a glass mug. We both watched the cream roiling in the coffee, unfolding like a flower. "But one day I snapped out of it."

"How do I get back to normal?" I asked her. "How do I stop from worrying about every goddamn thing?"

120

With great concentration, Nira flicked her cigarette against the rim of an ashtray. Then she looked up at me, her plan made. "From now on, you're absolutely not allowed to think about anything profound. If you want to get better, you're going to have to think about superficial things."

When she said this, I panicked. "Like what?" I said.

"The philosophy tea," she leaned forward, her smoke in my face.

"What philosophy tea?"

"Friday, dummy. It's supposed to be for prospective majors to talk to professors," she said. "From now on, you must only think about what you will wear to it and who you will seduce."

In my anguish, I stared at the Formica table, the flecks and filmy shapes there that almost seemed to form words. "I don't want to go," I said. The diner seemed horribly stuffy, air greasy with the smell of bacon.

121

"No way," she said. "You're going. You'll take a shower. We'll buy you a dress at the Salvation Army. You'll look fantastic."

WHEN FRIDAY MORNING came, I got my philosophy paper back with a D on it. The only comment was, "This is completely incoherent and shows no comprehension of the subject. Nor does it address the assigned topic." I hadn't remembered that there was an assigned topic. I had written the paper after Nira and I got back from the Blue Bonnet because she'd told me to finish it as quickly as possible. It was dangerous for me to dwell on Nietzsche.

First thing I did was find Nira in the library lounge. I didn't say anything, just handed her the paper. She read it quickly and then sighed. "This is so sincere. I told you, you have to have an attitude." But then she added, "Don't worry about it. You'll make good on the final paper. I promise." I flopped down next to her and she leaned toward me, the tips of her hair like upturned hooks. "There's only one thing to do now. We both have to get drunk." And so we went back to her house, sat on the floor of her room, listened to "Born To Be Wild" over and over, and passed a fifth of vodka back and forth. I think there was a period when we were crawling around on her carpet looking for something and giggling. Eventually, Nira said, "It's time for the tea."

She lent me one of her dresses—a shimmery '40s shift that was too tight and too short—and one of her pillbox hats that sat uncertainly on my piled-up hair. Next thing I knew, we were marching through the Black Forest singing "*Deutschland, Deutschland über Alles.*" Nira held onto her own hat, a fez, and gripped my arm with her other hand. Though we strode along the dirt road at a steady pace, I glimpsed things in snatches, as if we were running very fast. The mark of a heel frozen into the mud looked exactly like a D, and this made me laugh all the harder.

It took both of us to open the huge door of the philosophy department, and we nearly tumbled to the ground at the effort. Once inside, we stood snickering quietly and holding onto one another for balance. We could hear the faint chamber music coming from one of the rooms at the back of the mansion. We began stumbling in that direction, but then Nira stopped, her eyes fixed on the banister.

"You know, I've always, always wanted to slide down this thing," she said. Indeed, the banister was so smooth and wide, it seemed to have been made for that purpose.

"But people will be coming in the door," I said.

"Come on," she said, bounding up the stairs. I followed and helped her get her leg over the railing. She slid backwards down it, flew off the end, landed on her feet with a resounding thump, fell onto her butt and crawled out of my way. "Hurry," she said and I found myself scrambling astride the banister, as if there really was some reason I must hurry. The floor spun far below me, and the next thing I knew, I had slid down and was flying off the end and then— WHAM—collided with someone who collapsed under me in a tangle of arms and legs.

I'll never know if Nira had somehow arranged it, or if Mr. Shapiro, who I suppose was in the next room, had rushed out at the thunder of her landing and so just happened to be standing in front of the banister when I shot off its end.

In any case, I found myself on top of him. His glasses had come off and his eyes were rolling. For an instant, when I turned to see who I'd bagged, our faces were close and I smelled the spiciness of his breath. His body was pathetically bony under mine, and I had the impression I could have pinned him down as long

123

as I wanted. Instead, I climbed off him, found his glasses on the rug and handed them to him.

"I'm really sorry," I said. "Are you okay?"

He scrambled to his feet, stood unsteadily, and then ran for the coat rack. I guess he must have thought that, driven mad by my D, I had been waiting on the stairs to tackle him.

"Mr. Shapiro," I called, running behind him.

With his coat half on, he yanked open the front door and dove through it. By the time I got outside, he was loping down the road, and I stood on the porch and watched as he disappeared into the Black Forest.

MR. SHAPIRO NEVER mentioned our encounter. But when his eyes happened to fall on me in class, they fluttered away before I could meet his gaze.

He said that, if we liked, he would look at the first draft of our final papers, and so I handed mine in at the end of February. The best strategy, I thought, was to become an apologist for Nietzsche myself, but at the same time not to challenge Mr. Shapiro in his field of expertise. I decided to argue that, despite the claims of most scholars, Nietzsche was no sexist, but indeed the first feminist. As Nietzsche was a great misogynist, this proved easy.

I found quotes such as, "The perfect woman perpetrates literature as she perpetrates a small sin: as an experiment, in passing, looking around to see if anybody notices it." Also, there was, "Go to women? Then take the whip." I argued that Nietzsche didn't scorn women, he was merely disappointed when they failed to step out of their stereotypes. I cited his relationship with the free-thinking Lou Salomé and his intellectual partnership with his sister before she betrayed him.

When I got the paper back, it was ticked with check marks and little exclamations of "brilliant" and "very true." At the bottom he wrote, "Retype this, fix the spelling, and you'll have an A+ for the course." At the time I was quite pleased I'd finally impressed him; but now I wonder if perhaps he was just afraid to criticize me, lest I once again ambush him.

After the harsh winter, spring came with heartrending suddenness. The grass in the quad was fat and fine and brilliant green. The earth steamed. The river turned blue and blindingly bright where the sun hit it.

125

I dyed my hair. It hung all around my face and down my back in blue-black strings. I wore pink tights, gold slippers and polyester dresses. I joined the radicals in storming the administration building and later we retired to the campus coffee shop to discuss the ideas of Gandhi.

The leaves on the apple trees in the Black Forest had popped open, and the hard little fruits littered the grass like golf balls. One day, before class, I was sitting high up on a branch when the boy who smoked clove cigarettes passed under me. Without knowing beforehand I was going to do it, I yelled, "Hi." He looked up, confused. He was tall and gangly and his hair hung limply across his forehead the way it does only on the very rich. He wore an inside-out sweatshirt. The letters on the other side showed through faintly. They said, "Groton."

I pointed to his chest and said, "My little brother goes there."

He shielded his face with a hand and looked up at me. "Yeah?" he said.

I scrambled down the trunk and jumped to the ground. "Yeah," I said. He seemed just like my little brother, rather bland and good-natured and easily bossed. "You know what?" I said. "I think Shapiro is full of shit."

I had no idea what I meant by this, but he said, "You're right. I've heard him misquote Nietzsche, and I think he's entirely wrong about the politics."

126

Just then, Mr. Shapiro emerged from the pine trees at the edge of the orchard and we fell guiltily silent and stood not knowing what to say or where to look as he approached. He nodded to us as he scurried past, clutching his books like a painful tumor at his side. "We'll be up in a minute," called the clove boy. And then he half-whispered, "He didn't like my paper because I argued against him."

I couldn't answer. I couldn't take my eyes from the forlorn figure in flapping black clothes hobbling away from us. Something about him just then reminded me of the mad Nietzsche, who would sit quietly for hours and then suddenly erupt into screams.

I had almost forgotten about the screams. When I looked back at the clove boy, he was tossing his head to get the hair out of his eyes, waiting for me to say something. Behind him stretched a field of tall yellow grass, almost too bright to bear in the sun.

"Let's go," I said. I felt little for the clove boy except disdain. But as we ambled down the dirt road, he seemed to belong bobbing beside me, long limbs lithe with life, telling me how he couldn't wait for vacation, the sailing and the swimming and biking with bare feet—these things he would enjoy during what I knew would be the vapid span of a privileged summer.

UFOs

"IF THEY CAN send a man to the moon, why can't they send them all?" Someone says this to Jenny and for a while that's how she thinks it maybe should be: all the men on the moon, all the women on Earth. Maybe there would be mixers, but otherwise, no communication.

She'd been living with Dave since the spring, although she was never stupid enough to call him her boyfriend. To call Dave her boyfriend, or even to think it in her head, even to imagine, say, that she and Dave are at a malt shop sharing a soda through two straws, or that maybe he brought her a corsage when they went to the high school prom together—although, in real life, Jenny didn't meet him until college—even to think one thing like that or to imply it with a word like "boyfriend" would make Dave feel tied down, and when he feels tied down, he has a fit.

That's why she moves out—Dave's fits. Really, he has fits according to some inner schedule of his own that has nothing to do with her at all.

He has a pink, purple and green bowling ball he bought at a garage sale. His housemates call this his planet because he sometimes tries to stand on it and twirl around. Jenny can barely lift the thing, but when he's having a fit, he has been known to hurl it off the back porch.

The other thing he does is come up with theories. He'll take something you say, even something innocuous, and argue against you using theories that are intricately insane. He'll look things up in books, quote scientific formulas; he'll use insults if necessary.

Once, for instance, she was telling him that she was feeling guilty about the world. She was getting obsessed—talking about the same thing over and over again, going, "Dave, if the world's going to end, we shouldn't waste time trying to save it, but then if we think we shouldn't do anything, we won't, and then the world will end." They were sitting in Dave's kitchen, and maybe she'd been repeating the same thing for a long time, because Dave, who'd been just kind of nodding his head, suddenly hit the table with his fist real hard.

"You're not thinking, Jenny." She knew he took it personally when her logic was faulty. "Look, moral action depends on whether there's free will or not, right?" Then he proved there was no free will. It had

130

something to do with how they'd discovered that the universe wasn't just expanding, it was expanding and contracting, which meant that time repeats itself over and over again. "Look, will you just think this out? What you perceive as free will is only an illusion. Your life has already happened billions of times. So stop freaking out about what you should do, because you don't have any choice."

It seemed to her that if this was correct, then she was fated to agonize, too, but she didn't say anything because of the way he looked, so crazy pacing up and down talking to himself.

IT'S AFTER A particularly bad fit of Dave's that she finally moves out. They're watching the news and the news people are saying how America has invaded that Third World country and Jenny says, "I can't believe this. Those jerks."

Dave says, "Are you kidding? We should be bombing them into the ground." He starts on his bomb-them-into-the-ground theory. She knows this isn't really what he thinks. Really, in a way, Dave is even more anti-war than she is, because Jenny has given up on ending war. She thinks if you're going to have men on Planet Earth, you're going to have to get used to war; women putting up with men's war is, on a planetary scale, like Jenny putting up with Dave's fits.

But once a theory has taken over Dave, it doesn't matter what he really thinks. The theory comes out of him whether he agrees with it or not. It's an uncontrollable physical reaction, like vomiting.

So Jenny goes up to stay on Beth's farm. A few weeks ago, when school ended, Beth broke up with her boyfriend, and moved to Maine to take a lesbian lover and till the sweet earth with her shirt off.

Jenny is only at her house a few days before Dave calls. He doesn't exactly say he's sorry, not in so many words; instead, he tells her a story.

He says that what people think are falling stars are really UFOs landing. It was in one of these UFOs that he came to Planet Earth. He was just a baby, and the UFO dropped him off at his parents' house; they raised him as they would a human child.

Jenny says, "Oh, so you're not human then?"

"Sometimes I lose control," he says and changes the subject—he's decided he wants to come up to Beth's farm to hang out for a few days, if Jenny doesn't mind.

"Okay," she says, even though, officially, she's broken up with him and is supposed to be so mad that she isn't even speaking to him.

After her phone conversation with Dave, she says to Beth, "Oh, God, I know I've been complaining about Dave's theories, but now I sort of miss them." She says that sometimes she and Dave would stay up all night arguing theoretical points. "He said he isn't trying to be mean by always arguing against me; he's just trying to make me think things out. I know that's a patriarchal attitude, but maybe he has a point."

Beth has made iced herb tea and as she pours Jenny a glass she says, "Oh, don't fall for his crap." Beth says that men are just upside-down minotaurs—with human heads and the bodies of bulls. She read that somewhere. "They may appear to have very impressive minds, but they're at the mercy of their lower anatomy."

Then Beth and Jenny complain about men like they used to in the old days. The old days were two weeks ago, before school ended for the summer.

Once Jenny said to Beth, "I give up—I'm just going to become one of them. I'll just turn into a man, that's all."

Beth had been opposed this idea. She said, "Jenny, don't do it. They're screwing up the whole ecosystem."

Jenny had agreed with Beth, just to keep her company, even though she didn't believe that the death of the planet was men's fault. Really, the dying planet seemed just another of nature's sick jokes, like tying you to some guy who freaks out and throws bowling balls and really thinks it matters whether the universe is expanding or expanding and contracting.

WHEN DAVE ARRIVES, Jenny is alone in the cabin; Beth is at an anti-war demonstration.

Dave and his friend Paul have brought a piece of paper perforated into tiny squares, each square with a heart stamped on it. You put a piece of this paper into your mouth and it makes you realize that you love everybody, that everyone is really just the same, and that there's no reason why there shouldn't be peace on Planet Earth. Dave and Jenny talk about how you could slip this paper into the water of world leaders, and then they wouldn't want to have this war in the

Third World. Instead, all they'd want to do is play electric guitars, give each other backrubs, and crawl around on the floor of the U.N.

Since there's nothing to do on a farm without a TV set or anything, Jenny says maybe they should eat some of the paper. Besides, she would rather be with a dosed Dave than a straight Dave. If Dave is dosed, maybe it will be a little like the old days, when they first started sleeping together. Back then, they could communicate telepathically. Jenny would send Dave a message that she was coming to stay the night and when she got to his house the porch light would be on and he would be preparing his generic noodles and peanut butter dinner for her.

134   Jenny and Paul decide to split one of the squares of paper, but while she's cutting it off, she drops the sheet of paper in the sink and a whole corner of it gets wet. She cuts off the wet part and gives it to Dave: "Here, you want these? They probably won't do much."

The three of them begin walking down the road, away from Beth's cabin. After what seems a long time, they turn off onto a trail leading through a hallway of pine trees that smells like air freshener. Their trail leads to a lake ringed by trees.

"This is a very green planet," Dave says.

Jenny walks off by herself to crouch at the edge of the lake. She puts her fingers in the water, where they turn fat and light green. She steadies herself and leans over as far as she can, trying to see below the surface, but all she can make out is brown specks floating around, and below that, lacy seaweed. With her face so close to the surface, she notices that the water smells like dirty diapers.

She sits up again. The other two are gone. Nearby, the leaves on a tree wave like little hands.

Suddenly, she hears a cracking sound from the woods, and she jumps up to follow it. When she catches sight of Dave, he's trying to rip a limb off a tree. So far, he's managed to twist it enough so that a white crack runs along the black limb.

"What's wrong with you? You're going to get lost," she says.

"Lost?" he says, and she thinks he's making fun of her, like during his fits. Then she sees his face. There's something wrong with him. She takes him by his overall strap, which hangs down behind him like a tail. She feels that if she touches his skin, they'll be back together again.

135

She leads him along the twisting trail back to the lake, and there's Paul, lying on a rock.

She lets go of the overall strap. "Something's wrong with Dave," she says.

Just as she says this, Dave steps off a rock and walks into the lake. He stands up to his knees in the water. Joined to the real Dave at the knees is a reflected Dave, cut into little rippling strips that twitch whenever he moves. Jenny wades in after him and reaches out to grab one of his arms.

She sits on one rock, Dave in her arms; Paul sits on another, taking in the sun. Dave begins to cry. "Dad is dead," he sobs, though not crying like normal. It's more like his body is just jerking around.

Jenny holds him and says, "No he's not," and whispers over Dave's shoulder to Paul, "His father's just been put in the bin."

Dave leans against her and says, "Laugh, Jenny." She thinks this is supposed to mean "kiss," because he seems to be trying to aim his mouth at her.

She pushes his jaw sideways, the way you do with a dog that's trying to lick you, and his mouth lands on her ear.

"I was only trying to make you laugh," he whispers.

She wishes Paul weren't there because she's not sure whether he knows that she and Dave have broken up. Because she's not sure about Paul's perception of her and Dave's relationship, she doesn't know how to act. If Paul thinks that they're still together, then she should let Dave kiss her. But if Paul knows they've broken up, then she shouldn't.

So she's embarrassed when Dave says, "Are we back together, Jenny? Please can we just be back together?"

"Sure, Dave," she whispers.

WHEN IT STARTS to get dark, they steer Dave back to Beth's cabin and he heads straight into the tent that he set up by the garden. They leave him alone for an hour or so, but then Jenny starts to worry about that quiet tent and says to Paul, "I better go check on him."

When she crawls inside, Dave is lying under a sleeping bag. In the luna-moth green light, his bony face looks like an alien's.

"Are you okay?"

"I don't think so. I don't think I'm ever going to come back." His voice cracks when he says it and Jenny hopes he's not going to cry again. She thinks that because he can answer her he must be beginning to come down. She gets under the sleeping bag with him and strokes his hair.

She says, "Of course you will, in just a little while now."

Dave says he's been hearing voices all day and that most of the time when they were down by the lake, the voices told him Jenny was his enemy.

She thinks that eating all those squares of paper must have triggered some kind of psychotic thing in Dave. If his Dad could go crazy, then he could go crazy too. Dave must have crazy genes.

137

"If it hadn't been for you, I probably would have ended up in the hospital today," he says. "I guess I'm okay now. We can go inside if you want."

"Only if you want," she says.

"No, if you want."

"For God's sake, Dave."

So they stay.

JENNY MOVES CLOSER, putting her arm around his back. He gives off the animal smell of someone who's been crazy all day, and in each of his eyes is a white square, the reflection of the tent window.

Earlier, when they were sitting on little rickety chairs beside Beth's garden sharing a beer, he told her his dad was in the hospital. That's what he said, "hospital," so at first Jenny had thought his father had been hit by a car or something. Mental hospital, he'd explained.

All of a sudden she'd realized there were two Daves. This Dave—the one he became when he was alone with her—was the one she loved. When the other Dave was throwing a fit, yelling, pounding on tables, this one watched him from inside.

Now Jenny asks, "Why did they put him in there, your dad?"

"Last week, my mom said he couldn't stop crying; he kept saying he wanted to die. She didn't know what to do, so she put him in there for a while. We can get him out, though, if we want. She made sure." He falls silent and they lie there, the light in the tent fading to dark green.

138

THEY HEAR SWISHING noises coming toward them in the grass and Paul says through the tent, "You guys, there's a meteor shower out here."

They come out and sit on the hood of the car with everyone else.

"Look, there's one," Beth says, her finger following it downward. Her girlfriend, Chris, is sitting next to her.

"How was it?" Jenny asks, because she hasn't seen Beth since she left for the demonstration.

"Depressing," Beth says. "Hopeless."

Beth and Chris have on identical "No War" T-shirts, and when they put their arms around one another they look like twins. They're talking between themselves now. Paul is lying in the grass, watching the sky. Dave and Jenny sit with their legs dangling over the hood of the car, hips touching. Dave has on his leather jacket with the American flag painted on the back, and Jenny puts her arm around his starspangled shoulder.

ALIEN BEINGS FROM another world planted the seeds of intelligent life on Planet Earth, and this is how: they had sex with monkeys. When Dave says that, Jenny knows he's back to normal. They've been talking in the tent, and Dave has been feeling better, but when he starts coming up with theories, then she knows he's back to his old self.

She leans close to him and sniffs. "Are you sure you're not one of the aliens yourself? You don't smell like a human, you know. People are supposed to smell like antiperspirant."

"I don't need to wear antiperspirant. I've had my glands removed."

"I bet that's just what the aliens said to the monkeys." She thinks those aliens were probably smelly. They probably smelled like the weird food they brought from their planet. And the monkeys stunk too. On the whole, the conception of the human race must have been a pretty smelly process. She says, "Maybe our sweat smells exactly like what the alien and monkey smelled like when they were together."

Jenny and Dave do it—but still the theories are chattering through Dave's head, so that instead of thinking of having sex this particular time, he's think-

139

ing about the concept of sex. It seems to him that a penis is an anti-vagina; and a vagina, an anti-penis. If human beings use antiperspirant to mask the scent of their own conception, then they use their anti-penis or anti-vagina to bring it back. Furthermore, if we say that the vagina is X, then the penis would be -X. If what Dave feels during a screw is Y, what Jenny feels is -Y. What Dave feels in his anti-vagina is the exact and perfect opposite of what Jenny feels in her anti-penis.

DAVE HAS FINALLY fallen asleep, and his body on the tent floor—one thin arm curling before him, his legs bent—forms a hieroglyph. He shudders with every breath, as if sleeping were an effort, and sometimes he mutters, working out theories in his dreams. Between the bristles of his crew cut Jenny can see his scalp.

Since she's wearing only a T-shirt and sitting on the thin plastic of the tent floor, the twigs and pebbles and bent-down grass underneath the plastic stick into her hands, the back of her legs. When she lifts a hand, a pattern of indentations decorates her palm; as a kid, she thought this pattern formed letters in a secret language.

Out the window of the tent, the moon is full and the stars are brighter than she's ever seen. The stars are like points on a chart, some kind of graph that Jenny can't understand.

This is what Beth would say, she thinks: The monkeys were seduced by the spaceman's mathematical theories.

The monkeys had no way to argue when the spacemen, with their charts and graphs and logarithmic equations, proved that having sex with spacemen was necessary to the creation of a new species and the evolution of life on Planet Earth.

IN THE MIDDLE of the night, she leans over him. "Dave," she whispers, "are you asleep?"

After a bit, he says, "Of course not." He claims that he doesn't sleep; he just lies down and closes his eyes for eight hours to be polite.

"I can't sleep. I feel really hyper," she says. "I guess that stuff had a lot of speed in it. Do you have any gum or cigarettes or anything?"

"Yeah." He sits up, kicks off the sleeping bag, searches the pockets of his army-surplus backpack, and finally finds a crumpled pack of cigarettes. "These are the same ones from before, I think." He means from before they broke up.

She remembers: One day they rode double—on a kid's Sting Ray bike Dave had bought at a garage sale—into town and got the cigarettes. Then they walked back through the empty streets, smoking. For some reason, it had seemed like an adventure. Jenny imagines that some of the air from that day was trapped in the cigarette pack, that when he opens the pack, it will escape, mingling with the air they're breathing.

They go out and sit on the grass, and he lights a cigarette for her, and then one for himself. In the dark, the cigarettes turn them each into just a dot of light,

141

orange stars that glow brighter when they take a drag. Together they form a constellation of two.

The Dave she loves is the one from that day with the cigarettes. He understood her perfectly, as if her personality were a magic marble he held to his eye and saw a whole planet inside of.

He's thinking of that day at the beginning of the summer, too, though what he remembers is different. He walked down to the store alone and bought bread and milk and cigarettes while Jenny filled the baby pool they'd found in the backyard. Then they lay in the pool all afternoon. The tall grass had taken over the yard, so that you had to wade through it. The branches on the trees drooped with the weight of waxy, dark leaves. Behind them, the old house was covered in creepers, decaying in the heat, wood peeling away in giant splinters. The blue of the pool was hallucinatory. A cat sat in a wicker chair nearby, his saffron eyes half-shut.

Dave and Jenny had both been wearing cut-offs as swimsuits. Jenny slid down so that only her face, arms, breasts and knees showed above the water.

She said her arms and breasts were land rising out of the water; her knees were volcanic islands, uninhabitable. A beer can floating by became a space capsule that had just splashed down. They made ships out of leaves. They followed the adventures of one particular leaf: on board the brave crew searched for the lost land of Atlantis.

"Bleh," Jenny had said, "there's a dead ant on my shoulder. Get it off, will you?"

And he brushed it off, back into the water.

"That was one of our Atlantian ancestors. A superior race, though for some reason they all died out."

But it didn't really matter what she said or he said, what mattered was the way the hollows of her neck gathered the blue of the sky; the buttery orange of the cat watching them; the smell of the grass; the way he felt.

Now Jenny says, "Hey," and puts her hand on his shoulder. "I think I can see my reflection in your eyes, just from the porch light. I look all weird in there." She stares into one eye, at herself, he guesses. She touches his ear, as if adjusting something. He knows what she wants from him. It would be like swimming up to the surface from a long way down. It would require the saying of certain words, a magical spell that will bring back that moment in the pool.

143

He doesn't know how. She's still staring at him and it makes him nervous. It seems to him that what happened then just happened—there's nothing he can do to bring it back. He leans forward.

She watches as his head comes toward her. At first she thinks he's going to say something; to explain, finally, how he feels about her; to talk, for once, not about aliens or the universe, but about what's going on right here, right now on Planet Earth.

His face comes closer and she smells the cigarette on his breath; he says in a low, soft voice, "I'm going to figure it out."

And Jenny nods as if she understands what this means.

JENNY WAKES UP in the green afternoon of the tent; Dave is gone. Out the window, the sky is a blinding blue. She lifts the flap and crawls out. At the other end of the field, Beth, wearing a bathrobe, sunglasses and a floppy straw hat, is watering her garden with a pink can. When she sees Jenny, she walks over, wiping her hands on the terry cloth. "We've got to go rowing," she says. "That's the plan for today. There's this boat tied up on the lake, and I'm sure whoever owns it won't mind if we borrow it. Dave's already down there."

There are two oars in the boat, but it's hard to row because the lake is full of green scum. The scum makes the lake very green, and the green lake makes everything look prehistoric. Deep in the woods, at this very moment, a spaceship could have just landed; deep in the woods, the aliens could be seducing the monkeys.

Beth determines that the scum is actually alive. It's algae. She says she's rethinking the whole thing—maybe they should be in the water instead of in the boat.

"After all," says Beth, "the algae is our mother. It turned into us a long time ago." She says she read that somewhere. Beth says, "Algae turning into humans is not what I call evolution—that's what I call de-evolution." She touches some of the algae, and says, "Mom." Then she jumps into the water, disappears for a minute, and comes up green and slimy.

Jenny can't decide whether to stay in the boat or to jump into the slime with Beth—she's not like Beth, who's not afraid of nature, no matter how slimy.

144

As a sort of compromise, she slides over the edge of the boat on her stomach. She keeps her arms and head in the boat, but from her waist down, she's in the lake. Jenny can feel the slime swirling around her stomach and legs—frighteningly alive, trying to suck her farther in.

Beth splashes her and says, "Jenny's a mermaid. Jenny, I looked at you underwater and your legs have turned into a tail. Come in all the way. Don't be scared."

Jenny says, "No, no, it's gross."

Meanwhile, Dave stays in the boat, theories spouting from his mouth as if logic is what keeps him from sinking into the glistening green goo.

"As far as I'm concerned," he says, "humans are better than algae. For one thing, human cell structure is more complicated than algae cell structure, and in terms of life, or evolution, that is, complication is superiority."

He cites the equation that proves this, argues in favor of cell division, brings in theories of mutation, theories about the power of pyramids in preserving living tissue, theories about alien mutilation of cattle.

While the theories come out of his mouth, Beth lies in the slime. She has an algae belly, algae hair, algae arms. She is saying, "Mom, Mom, Mom, Mom."

They each of them know about creation, about how you should live and what you should believe, Jenny thinks. But she can't decide what's right—whether Dave's a patriarchal pig as Beth would say behind his back, or whether he's a genius who's trying his best to

145

be nice to her. Her stomach begins to hurt terribly because of the way she's lying over the gunwale of the boat—it feels like she's being cut in half there—but for the life of her she can't decide whether to go in or come out.

"JENNY," HE SAYS, "Jenny," as he walks up to her, and she thinks how strange and good he looks, all loose limbs and too-big hands, patched pants and black eyes. Jenny's sitting in a folding chair by the garden, doing nothing but breathing the fine air.

"I've been thinking," he says, and the way he sounds, she assumes he's finally going to tell her how he feels. For an instant, with Dave standing against the bright blue sky and Jenny waiting, it seemed as if they are poised to confess everything to each other.

But then he starts pacing back and forth in front of her chair and she can tell he's in the throes of a theory. His hands are twirling; his mouth is moving. "Everything points to it," he says. Then he begins enumerating on his fingers: "The weather's getting weird, the animals are acting strange, the political situation, the war. It's time to leave."

"Leave where?" Jenny says. She keeps her face straight, to hide her terrible disappointment.

"The planet," he says. The aliens came to Earth from a universe that knows only love, he explains. In that realm, love is pure—not mixed as it is here with other feelings. Now it's time for the right people to get together for the return trip. He doesn't say whether this will require actual intergalactic travel, or merely a subtle change of mind; whether the Love Universe is real, or merely Planet Earth seen through other eyes.

Still standing, he takes her hand. "See the lines on your fingertip? They're like that UFO landing field in the Nazca desert." Jenny knows what he's referring to: Dave has a book with actual documentation of the aliens' visit to Planet Earth. One photograph shows a monkey limned so large in the desert it could only be seen from a plane—or from a spaceship. The book says the aliens made these huge drawings in the ground so they'd know where to land when they returned to Earth.

"What does that have to do with it?" Jenny says. She keeps thinking of his father in that institution, standing at the window, waiting for Dave's mother to come take him home. Inside this Dave who is raving at her now, the real Dave, the one she loves, is silent, sealed behind glass.

147

"We're descended from the spaceman and the monkey, right? So that means the spaceman half of ourselves leaves clues about the way back to the Love Universe—I mean, maybe we secretly know it, genetic memory, but we've just got to crack the code. I've got this feeling the signs will especially be in the things people usually ignore—you know, the dialogue in monster movies, instructions that come with blenders, the fortunes in Bazooka Joe comics."

And as Dave paces, talking on and on about the Love Universe, Jenny wonders whether, in his own way, he *is* trying to tell her how he feels; like the aliens, he communicates only in clues, hints, metaphors of such grand design that she never will unravel his meaning, or glimpse the secret universe of his emotion. Maybe it's right at that moment that she makes her decision about him.

He leans over her. "So we should go to Peru, really, to check this out," he says, or something like that. She's not following his words anymore.

"I don't want to go anywhere. I'm tired," she says, but he's already out of earshot. He's running toward the tent, leaving a silvery pattern of bent-down stalks in the endless, ancient field of grass.

The Monument

I DON'T KNOW why people talk in other towns and not in ours. I don't know why everything here is silent. The lawns around our houses, for instance, are as green and silent as pools of water— except, at night, for the sound of crickets, which I sometimes mistake for the sound of old people rocking in wicker chairs on the front porch, a sound from my childhood.

Sometimes I forget and think my childhood was here, in this town. Certainly the grass in this town is the same color as the grass of my childhood; the green of sea glass on its underside, a color I cannot describe on top.

You may wonder how, in our silent town, we get by day after day without a word. The secret, I believe, is in our strict adherence to habit. For instance, whenever we—this other and myself—go to the diner in town, the counter man always brings us the same thing—black coffee—without our having to say a word. Perhaps he knows to bring us coffee because long ago, once, or perhaps several times, we ordered it with words, as people do in other towns. But if that were the case, then surely I would remember saying words, and I remember saying nothing.

Our adherence to habit also makes talk unnecessary in matters of household logistics. We—this other and myself—do not need to tell each other where we have put something, keys say, or at what time a certain domestic ritual will occur, supper say, because our habits are so exactly the same every day, every year, that nothing is left to chance.

150

I often feel that this pattern we follow—the trail of our feet through the house, the amount and placement of our cigarette ashes, the rhythm of our breathing even—corresponds in some way I cannot exactly express to the map of the town we have hung on our wall. Perhaps it is that we have learned our routine from the layout of our town's buildings and roads; or perhaps it is the other way around. Perhaps the town depends on our silence for its own silence, and if we were to talk, the spell that binds him and me and holds the town all around us would be broken.

When I say the word "spell" I am thinking of the old men in the diner. There is nothing about these old men to suggest that they are anything other than farmers; nothing about their behavior is out of the ordinary, each hunched over a plate of food or a newspaper, each a lump of worn denim. Still, I often get the feeling that there is a silent communion among them, that they are a secret society or a council of elders, that it is these old men who hold our town to its silence. Then I look down into my black coffee and discover my own reflection there. That my coffee is a kind of mirror seems like something they have arranged.

I wish I could say I don't miss talking, that it serves no purpose. But to tell you the truth, even in all this silence, my mind is never quiet; I am always talking to him inside. Always keeping it in is not pleasant, for when something is thought and not said a pressure builds.

Perhaps because of this pressure, I am always imagining what we might say to one another if we lived in a town where people did talk. We might say, for instance, "I will never leave you; I would not exist without you." We might even say it in French. But, after all, we moved to this town to avoid such things.

Did I tell you I grew up in this town? Back then, I had a rag doll with a piece of abalone shell sewn over its face. The shell looked like a winter sky or oil spilled on water.

When she gave me the doll, my mother told me—not with words, but with implication, or perhaps not with implication either, and it was only something I imagined—that there is a painless place where one can live and can expect peace; where, if nothing's very good, it's never very bad either.

When I looked into the shiny shell that was my

151

doll's face all I could see was a vague shadow, the shadow of my own head. I used to imagine what her face might look like—whether it was painted on or blank under that shell—but I never bothered to cut the shell off.

In the summer, at night, we lie on top of the sheets, smoking, until it is time to sleep. Because of the moon, I suppose, the light at these times is strange; the smoke, rising silently from the cigarette in my hand, illuminated, looks like a veil hanging between us.

It is then, through that veil, that I really look at him. His skin is so pale that it glows a little in this strange light. He has little black hairs all over him. These hairs are like letters from an alphabet I don't know. There he is, spread out before me, like a page of a book written in a language I can't read.

When I see him like that, I think, for some reason, of the monument in the center of town. It is a rock, as tall as I am, with no words written on it. Perhaps it is not a monument at all, but just a rock that was too big to move.

In the summer, during the day, I walk down to the road to watch the cars that pass every once in a while. Mostly, these cars come from other towns, and so I am hoping to see the people inside, to see them talking. But for some reason, cars always pass through our town with their windows rolled up. When I try to look in through the windows as the car drives toward me, all I can see is reflection—of trees, of fields, of the few, far-flung buildings of our town, of myself—sliding over the surface of the car.

It is the same with the stream that runs by our house, and, farther down, past the town. I try to look into the water, for although I am so familiar with the stream that it is like a thing from my childhood, I have the feeling that something quite unfamiliar is living under its surface. In that green world, something hovers, something darts around.

All I can see of the stream is its surface. No, that's wrong, I can't see the surface either; what I see is my own world reflected back—the trees, the sky, a shadow that's my head—a reflection that's hiding, like a veil laid on the water, that other world below.

These past seven nights I have had the same dream. We—this other and myself—are lying on the green under the monument, or rock, at the center of town.

In this dream, there is something I must say to him that I can't hold in any longer. As I open my mouth, as I draw my breath, as I make the first sound, the town around me grows blurry, warped, puckered. As I say what I must say to him, I know that what I had taken to be a town is really only a reflection, sliding over the surface of I don't know what.

HIGH
RISK
BOOKS

To order HIGH RISK Books / Serpent's Tail:
(US) 212-274-8981   (UK) 071-354-1949